VIRAGO
MODERN CLASSICS
575

Rumer Godden (1907–98) was the acclaimed author of over sixty works of fiction and non-fiction for adults and children. Born in England, she and her siblings grew up in Narayanganj, India, and she later spent many years living in Calcutta and Kashmir. Several of her novels were made into films, including *Black Narcissus*, *The Greengage Summer* and *The River*, which was filmed by Jean Renoir. She was appointed OBE in 1993.

T0349217

A FUGUE IN TIME

Rumer Godden

VIRAGO

This paperback edition published in 2013 by Virago Press
First published in the United States in 1945 by the Curtis Publishing Company

12

A CIP catalogue record for this book is available from the British Library.

ISBN 978-1-84408-857-7

Typeset in Goudy by M Rules
Printed and bound in Great Britain by Clays Ltd, Elcograf S.p.A.

Papers used by Virago are from well-managed forests
and other responsible sources.

MIX
Paper | Supporting
responsible forestry
FSC
www.fsc.org   FSC® C104740

Virago Press
An imprint of
Little, Brown Book Group
Carmelite House
50 Victoria Embankment
London EC4Y 0DZ

The authorised representative
in the EEA is
Hachette Ireland
8 Castlecourt Centre
Dublin 15, D15 XTP3, Ireland
(email: info@hbgi.ie)

An Hachette UK Company
www.hachette.co.uk

www.virago.co.uk

To Miss Grace Underwood

*Without whose unfailing help and memory
it would have been very hard
to write this book*

... Two, three or four simultaneous melodies which are constantly on the move, each going its own independent way. For this reason the underlying harmony is often hard to decipher, being veiled by a maze of passing notes and suspensions ... Often chords are incomplete; only two tones are sounded so that one's imagination has to fill in the missing third tone.

> *A sentence describing Bach's fugues, written by*
> LAWRENCE ABBOT

And for Rolls personally, the poem he found: –
Home is where one starts from. As we grow older
The world becomes stranger, the pattern more
   complicated
Of dead and living. Not the intense moment
Isolated, with no before and after,
But a lifetime burning in every moment
And not the lifetime of one man only
But of old stones that cannot be deciphered,
There is a time for the evening under starlight,
A time for the evening under lamplight
(The evening with the photograph album).
Love is most nearly itself
When here and now cease to matter.
Old men ought to be explorers
Here or there does not matter
We must be still and still moving
Into another intensity
For a further union, a deeper communion ...
... In my end is my beginning.

T. S. ELIOT: 'East Coker'

Man that is born of a woman hath but a short time to live ... He cometh up, and is cut down, like a flower; he fleeth as it were a shadow, and never continueth in one stay.

Children and the fruit of the womb are an heritage and gift ... Like as the arrows in the hand of the giant: even so are the young children.

The Book of Common Prayer

CONTENTS

INVENTORY

The house, it seems, is more important than the characters. 'In me you exist,' says the house.

For almost a hundred years, for ninety-nine years, it has enhanced, embraced and sheltered the family, but there is no doubt that it can go on without them. 'Well,' the family might have retorted, 'we can go on without you.' There should be no question of retorts, nor of acrimony. The house and family are at their best and most gracious together.

The question of their parting had arisen. The lease was up. 'And the owners are not prepared to renew,' said Mr Willoughby, putting his despatch case on the table.

Rolls Dane – old General Sir Roland Ironmonger Dane, K.C.B., D.S.O. – looked at young Mr Willoughby with dislike. 'Not renew!' he said.

A lease of this sort, a ninety-nine years' tenancy, was a most unsatisfactory sort of lease, explained Mr Willoughby. He himself always advised against leases of this sort. The tenant was always the loser, all assets accrued to the owner, who in this case was not prepared to renew ...

'You need not say that again,' said Rolls.

Leases run for ninety-nine years; no more. Was that because, after a hundred years, some change takes place? A hundred years. A century. That had a ring about it. Rolls remembered the turn of the century. Before you were born, Rolls could have said to young Mr Willoughby, whom he disliked. New Year, nineteen hundred. He had been at a banquet. He remembered bells ringing and toasts and flags. There had been a war then too, a banquet in wartime was difficult to reconcile but he was, he confirmed, at a banquet. Wars then were not all-pervading; in any case things continue in spite of perpetual wars. He remembered too his first century at cricket; a spectacular one: sun on grass – small white figures and huge surrounding stands – a small thunder of clapping. Rolls's mind liked easy familiar phrases for his memories. He remembered, though not with the same pleasure, a fairy tale, a princess who fell asleep for a hundred years, in a spell. Rolls would have said 'Pshaw!' to a spell, but it was there all the same in his mind.

'Will they sell?' he asked abruptly.

'You wouldn't want to buy just now?' said young Mr Willoughby. He was Willoughby of Willoughby, Paxton, Low and Willoughby, who had been solicitors to the family for the lifetime of the firm. 'Besides,' said Mr Willoughby, 'I hear it is to be pulled down.'

But they can't pull down my house! cried Rolls – but he cried it silently because he was perfectly sensible of the fact that they could and that it was not his house. He was sensible and at the same time he was outraged. Outraged, he said in a voice that was muffled for all its calm: 'I don't want the family to go out of the house.'

The only remaining family was Rolls himself but Mr Willoughby could hardly point that out. He wondered what there was slightly unusual in the sentence Rolls had just said and presently, pondering, he thought it would have been more usual if Rolls had said 'I don't want the house to go out of the family.' Families possessed houses – not houses the family. 'We could try for a lease of occupation,' said Mr Willoughby. 'But I am afraid it would not be for long, say six months or a year, possibly for the duration.'

Six months. A year. The duration of the war, this war. Ninety-nine years. 'It is all comparative,' said Rolls, sitting heavily in his chair. 'Strictly comparative' – and every fibre of him, though he betrayed nothing to Mr Willoughby, cried out: Don't disturb me. Don't disturb me now. I don't want to be disturbed.

How the old boy can want to live on alone in that great barracks of a place! said Mr Willoughby's face behind his glasses, though his lips politely said nothing. How can you want to? it said.

Rolls, if he had heard, might have answered: Because there I can live. I have existed a considerable time, Mr Willoughby, Rolls might have said. And I am amazed to find for how little of that existence I have lived. You know the circumstances of my retirement, Mr Willoughby, Rolls might have said with his moustache and eyebrows bristling – and his eyebrows were nearly as thick as his moustache. They were unfailingly public. There was plenty of mud – and stones. I minded then. Now I have only this to say about its compulsion: For the first time since I was sent to school perhaps, I am in possession of my own life, and I intend to do, in its remaining time, exactly as I choose. I *intended*, he had to correct himself sadly. *Footfalls echo in the memory*, Mr Willoughby, and you offer me a lease of occupation.

He tried to remind himself that that was his true status: he was a tenant, an occupier – that is what all of us are. Anything we hold is on a lease – and a precious tenuous one, thought Rolls; but all the same he was outraged and angry and he disliked young Mr Willoughby more and more every minute and he refused to be reminded of anything he did not want to know.

'How long have we got?' he asked.

'The lease runs out on the fifteenth of December of this year,' said Mr Willoughby.

There is in London a Wiltshire Square, a Wiltshire Crescent, a Wiltshire Road; Wiltshire Gardens and Wiltshire Place; the house is Number 99 Wiltshire Place.

In the house the past is present.

It is the only house on the Place that has a plane-tree in the garden; for many years a Jewish family live next door and every year on the Feast of Tabernacles they ask for branches of the tree and build a little *sukkoth* on their balcony. All the houses have balconies, long ones across the French doors of the drawing-rooms at the back, and all the balconies have scrolled iron steps that lead down into the garden. The gardens are narrow and long, various in their stages of cultivation and neglect, heavily sooted as well. The gardens have an unmistakable London smell from the closed-in walls, and the earth that is heavy and old, long-undisturbed; the smell has soot in it too, and buried leaves, and the ashes of bonfires, and the smell of cat; any child, sent out to play, comes in with that smell; it is part of the memory of Selina and Rolls and the other children and Lark. The Jewish children, in their generations, play rounders in their garden; and the sound of their ball on the bat comes over the wall. The gardens have flowers; in the spring they have lilies of the valley and syringas; in the summer they have lime-flowers from the trees along their back walls; in the autumn there are Michaelmas daisies, at which time there are also bonfires that send a leaf-smelling country-smelling smoke out towards the road; in the winter there is nothing in the gardens but a colder smell of cats and soot and old decaying leaves. All these the houses have in common, but it is only Number 99 that has the tree.

The roots of the plane-tree are under the house. Rolls liked to fancy, sometimes, lately, that the plane-tree was himself. Its roots are in the house and so are mine, he said.

'You could find another house,' Mr Willoughby had suggested.

'I could but I would not,' Rolls had answered, 'and where could I find another tree?' . . . I am that tree, said Rolls.

He flattered himself. The plane-tree is more than Rolls, as is another tree of which Rolls truly is a part; it is a tree drawn on parchment, framed and hung over the chest in the hall by the grandfather clock. Selina draws it, marking the Danes in their places as they are born and die, making a demarcation line in red ink for the time they come to live in the house in the autumn of eighteen forty-one.

'We existed before you, you see,' the family might have said to the house; and the house, in its tickings, its rustlings, its creakings as its beams grow hot, grow cold – as the ashes fall in its grates, as its doorbells ring, as the trains in passing underneath it vibrate in its walls, as footsteps run up and down the stairs – as dusters are shaken, carpets beaten, beds turned down and dishes washed – as windows are opened or shut, blinds drawn up, pulled down – as the tap runs and is silent, as the lavatory is flushed – as the piano is played and books are taken down from the shelf, and brushes picked up and then laid down again on the dressing-table, and flowers are arranged in a vase – as the medicine bottle is shaken; as, with infinite delicate care, the spillikins are lifted in the children's game – as the mice run under the wainscot – the house might steadfastly reply, 'I know! I know. All the same, in me you exist.'

The tickings of the grandfather clock in the hall make swift and many alterations in the parchment tree, while the changes in the plane-tree are seasonal: In Rolls's whole lifetime it only grows a little taller, thicker, more leafy in summer perhaps. Its leaves bud and turn green and dry and fall and bud again. Rolls has altered from Roly the baby, and the little boy with the pudding-basin hair-cut, to Rollo the schoolboy and young blade; from Rollo the serious soldier to Rolls the general, the governor; and from that Rolls, who seemed so fossilized that he could never change, to Rolls the old man in the armchair who did not want to be disturbed.

The Place itself has subdued London colours: the houses, detached in pairs, are cream-grey stucco, their inner division marked by a waterpipe that goes up over their slated roofs among their ornamental chimneypots and down the houses on the garden side. In sunlight the slates are pale, in wet weather a pigeon-purple, and, down below, the dark asphalt of the road, the paler gutters, the still paler paving-stones, repeat, over and over again, the same cautious note.

On the opposite side of the Place is the church and convent of St Benedict, built in an enclosure that has more limetrees and asphalt walks and gravestones; it has heavy green railings that are afterwards taken away. St Benedict's vicarage shuts off the bottom of the Place. The steeple of the church has a brass-balled weathercock and it and the cross above the convent seem to fill the narrow space of sky, but the two pinnacles give to the houses their proper perspective of height and save the Place from the sense of imprisonment of other London streets. The church, in its time, has influenced, dominated, the life of the Place: it is stronger in Griselda's day, strong in Selina's, but it has never given Selina a sense of proportion and Griselda frequently feels imprisoned. Now, above the houses and the cross and the spire with its cock, floated the barrage balloons.

The sound of the church clock comes into the house; in peacetime the convent bell sounds there as well and the nuns walk in the enclosure under the limes where now only the occasional shape of a priest in a cassock and biretta can be seen hurrying through on his way from the vicarage to the church. In peacetime, every day, a Sister with a dozen infant orphans on reins, the bundle of reins tied to a ring in her hands, comes slowly out of the gridded convent door, slowly down the steps, and slowly, slowly, with these twelve impediments to her locomotion, sets off towards the Park.

All the houses in the Place are built alike; they stand in a row opposite the church and convent, and they are joined in pairs through their dining- and drawing-room walls and separated by area paths that lead down steps between walls to their back doors, low down in the house side.

The kitchens are basement; the servants' sitting-rooms are in the basement fronts and there, all along the Place, except at Number 5 which is a hostel, the curtains are uniformly, meticulously drawn to a distance of three feet and a table of pot plants put between them. Number 61, later, has a sewing machine instead and Number 17, for some time, a perambulator. The kitchen windows at Number 99 are further shaded by the plane-tree and by creepers that give a green reflection to the metal dishcovers with the dolphin handles in summer, and darker shadows to the room in winter. The servants live in a submerged gloom and they mostly have thin faces and sallow skins, though Mrs Proutie, for forty-seven years the cook, remains rosy and huge; she says it is from eating and handling so much good butcher's meat. She dies of blood pressure in the summer of 'eighty-seven.

The kitchen and its range and boiler with its cumbrous thick painted pipes is the core of the house; the burning of the fire, the boiling of the water, keep a warmth and continuity that is like breathing; when the range is raked it can be heard all over the house, and when it is stoked-up and the dampers are opened, cleaned, freshed and strengthened, it is so lusty that it is no surprise that, with it and the fires upstairs, a ton of coal is needed every week. The coal comes on a dray; the horses stand with their nosebags on; the coal sacks are hung one after the other along the iron rail down the centre of the dray as the men go backwards and forwards, emptying a stream of coal into the manhole that leads straight from the pavement to the coal-hole behind the kitchen. If it rains on the day the coal comes, the dray, the men and the horses are streaked and glistening with black and the coal shines and it is understandable that it is called 'black diamonds'; on a sunny day the horses and men smell strongly; when it is snow and the snow is bad the men have sacks over their backs and shoulders, and gravel is put down on the road to prevent the horses slipping. 'Gravel?' says little Verity, Rolls's great-great-nephew in the bad winter of nineteen forty-seven. 'Gravel? It isn't gravel, it is grapenuts.'

The kitchen fire breathes and the kitchen is living in the same way that the chrysanthemums in pots along its window-sill are living. The kitchen smells of them; even when they are not in flower they seem to scent the air. The air is hardly fresh but it is comfortable; it has a warm pungent smell flavoured with the flowers, and cinders and onions and nutmeg and starch and warm linen and ginger and coffee from the grinder on the corner of the dresser; like the garden, the kitchen smells a little of cat, but not of cats departed, of live cat. There was a present cat, lying at the table-leg, sunk in the mat, sunk in its bones, opening a little and shutting a little its eyes at the slit of the fire; it was just sufficiently awake to lift its purr into the morning.

'I am the house cat,' said the purr.

An echo comes from under the roots of the plane-tree. 'I am the house dog.' This echo is immediate and firm, in a jealous, small and certain-centred pug voice, but the twisting of the plane-tree roots, and the leaves that are banked up on them, hide even the mound of its grave.

'I am the house cat.'

'Well, I am the house dog.'

Outside the kitchen, in the passage that leads to the cellars, the scullery and the butler's pantry – outside the kitchen is a row of bells each numbered and lettered for the rooms upstairs. Three generations of butlers have answered those bells, each in a black coat, his feelings repressed behind his face, each using the same salvers, a pair presented to the Eye by the office staff on his marriage, heavy silver with his crest, a bird with an ear of wheat in its beak, in the centre. The butlers carry the same salvers, the same tea-tray, set the same dinner table, answer the same bells. As the house is lived in, it absorbs them a little – colours them: Slater is more human than Athay; Proutie than Slater – Proutie, nephew of the fat tyrannical cook, comes to work in the house early, as a boy.

Proutie was in the house still. He came down in the raw foggy morning to unlock the doors and let the cat out and let Mrs Crabbe the charwoman in. Proutie, Mrs Crabbe, the cat, the range and boiler and the chrysanthemums were all that were left of the denizens that inhabit the basement.

The stairs go up, oilclothed, brass-bound; steep, up to the ground floor that like most London ground floors is not on the ground at all but raised up from the street and from the garden; the stairs up to it are so designed that it is nearly impossible to carry heavy trays from the basement up them, but heavy trays are carried up them several times a day.

The ground floor is a different world. To begin with, it is infinitely more spacious, which is extraordinary because the house is the same width and breadth up all its height. The basement stairs are hidden by cream-painted banisters and a mahogany hand-rail that rises with serpentine twists up the well of the stairs. Grizel, when she arrives from America, remarks that stairs in a house are like highways in a country, exciting when they are unknown, soon familiar, linking all parts of it together, making them accessible and plain. Perhaps that accounts for the enormous traffic on these stairs, the continual endless going and flowing and hastening and toiling up and down them. The

carpet, the third carpet, for carpets like butlers wear out, is trod-
den nearly threadbare in places: the brass rods that fasten it are
thinned and fine with polishing; there is no need to polish the
hand rail, the hands do that, though the children leave marks
that are sticky: Roly sticks a lump of toffee under the rail in the
crack where it meets the banister; Lark finds it and recognizes it
as toffee eight years later; very faintly it still tastes like toffee.
The hall-and-stair paper is blue, a satin paper that the Eye buys
in ambitious extravagance; like most of his investments the
paper turns out well; in its hundred years it has only faded and
soiled to a pleasant Wedgwood blue. The Danes are good at
making investments, careers and money; they are faithful lovers
but keep their heads in love; Selina keeps hers so well that she
never falls in love.

On the ground floor an inner hall opens into an outer, a
vestibule that holds the front door with its wire cage for letters,
a doormat, a Kirman rug in a vase pattern of blue and green,
a hatrack, a chest with a blue-and-white china bowl for cards,
the family tree illuminated in a frame, and the grandfather
clock.

It leads in a chorus the clocks all over the house, and con-
nects them with the clocks outside, the church clock and other
clocks in spires and towers, as its chime is too big for an ordinary
house clock. It is always a second later than St Benedict's. Last
in the chorus by any number of minutes is the cuckoo clock on
the nursery landing; it breaks at last but when it breaks it has not
been required for more than thirty years. There are no more
children in the nursery.

There are three doors on the ground floor, doors with white
handles and white china door-plates embossed with gold

forget-me-nots and roses. They lead to the dining-room, the drawing-room and the study.

In the dining-room the peacock curtains are drawn; the curtains formerly are dark green but Selina changes them when the craze for changes comes, when she is given to wearing trailing dresses of olive-green and pale blue. Now in the morning dusk the ticking of the black marble clock on the mantelpiece fills the room. A dim daylight shines on the chains of the pictures that, gilt-framed, gilt-chained, are family portraits hung along the walls; the daylight picks up in them a patch of steel, of red velvet, a glove or a sash: it rests on the back of a greyhound, on a greengage; but nothing shows properly, nothing is clear in the room but the ticking of the clock. The table glimmers and the backs of chairs; even the smell is confused; there is a smell of old flowers and coal and of wax polish and, from the sideboard, of wine spilt on wood, and vinegar and nutmeg and chutney and, like an echo, of hot meat and cauliflower. A mouse runs across the table; its feet on the wood in the quiet are louder than the clock, and because they make an uneven sound, they break the quiet. It takes a crumb and scurries down onto the hearthrug and away.

In the drawing-room the curtains are not drawn and the light creeps into the room through the slats of the Venetian blinds. The drawing-room has a white wallpaper patterned in gold with bunches of poppies and barley-sheaves; it has sofas and armchairs with graceful black-and-gilt legs and they are upholstered in a scarlet damask patterned in diamonds. In eighteen sixty, after the Battle of Magenta, Griselda buys Lena a dress of magenta watered silk; she can never wear it in this room. There is a grey carpet with black and pale-pink roses, a white sheepskin hearthrug, a mantelpiece with white fluted marble sides and on it another clock in a glass case, a clock of painted Dresden china with a china shepherdess asleep on its top in a china meadow. There are long curtains of lace, fine, white and embroidered with fern-leaves. There is a carved walnut table from Cashmere. It is from the Great Exhibition. 'A mad idea. The hooligans will ruin the Park,' says the Eye when it first is mooted. 'Not an idea, a vision!' says Griselda with shining eyes. There is a crystal in the chandelier that sings, gives out a chime whenever a certain note is struck on the piano, or when a voice in singing reaches top D. There are many songs in the house: popular songs and hymns and carols; sentimental evening ballads; the songs Lark studies when at last she is given lessons; there are nursery songs and rhymes; and there are poems.

There was a poem in a book left open on the landing book-case. Rolls left it there when he went up to go to bed.

He left the study terribly untidy. Now that there was no staff, only Proutie and Mrs Crabbe, Rolls imagined he looked after himself, but after years of batmen, Indian bearers, valets and aides, he was not good at it. Proutie left him a kettle on the hob to make himself a hot toddy before he went up to bed; Rolls had put the kettle down on the carpet and made a dark brown ring. The glass, with the spoon and a piece of lemon in it, was in the fender; the evening paper and a cushion that Rolls had tried for his stiff back were on the floor.

The curtains in the study are drawn back, the light is bleak but clear. The narrow room, built up on its ground floor plinth, seems to be riding into the branches of the plane-tree. For the rest, the study is an uninviting room with something ambitious in the importance of the desk put halfway across it, and the grey-green walls, the maroon carpet, the black sheepskin rugs, the bookcases full of heavy ornamental books, the black marble mantelpiece and the clock that is a twin of the clock in the dining-room. There is a safe, a bust of Claudius Caesar crowned with laurel, and a picture.

It is light enough to see the picture. It is a peculiarly gracious picture in a narrow silver frame. It is painted on ivory on a background of grey trees and pillars that belong to an imaginary pavilion, Grecian, as are the dresses; it is of a young woman and a group of children, a large group of children: *Mrs Griselda Dane, wife of John Ironmonger Dane Esq., and their children: Pelham, John Robert, Lionel, James, Selwyn, Selina, Frederick, Elizabeth, and Rollo. 1861.* Visitors are always surprised to see, on looking into the picture, that Frederick, Elizabeth and Rollo are all of the same size. There is an explanation for that: the first two are twins, Rollo is painted in afterwards.

The sizes are recorded and the names repeated in pencilled handwriting, the Eye's handwriting, still faintly to be read, on the blue hall wall by the dining-room door: there the height of every child at two and five and ten years old is recorded in his neat small writing; Rollo is the tallest of the boys, Pelham the shortest; the twins are not recorded after five years old; and in the corner by the lacquer cabinet is another height marked by a crooked line and a name in big round writing quite different from the Eye's: *Lark*.

There is no Lark in the picture. There is not, anywhere in the house, a picture of Lark.

Though it is painted with deliberate stillness, styled, the picture seems alive in the room; it, and the litter left by Rolls, and the branches of the plane-tree that are reflected in their movement through the window-panes, onto the picture-glass.

Rolls, last night, was looking at the picture, looking at Griselda's eyes; at the important simper on Selina's lips; at the well-set-up sturdy little boys; at the shuttlecock and bunch of roses held by Freddie and Elizabeth; at his own head as it was when he was Roly with his hair cut round in a pudding-basin shape. He looked at himself and he asked a question. There was nothing in that; when he is that little boy he perpetually asks questions; later he ceased to question and to wonder.

Why? asked Rolls. Because I knew everything? Was always right? Hadn't the wit to be uncertain? Now, once again, he tingled with questioning as had that eager little boy. Can one remember before one is born? No, manifestly not. But … said Rolls looking at the picture. But I do remember, and I experience what happens; not only what happens when I was not there, but what was not there at all. What did not happen. What only might have been. *Might have been.* At the very words this new revivifying warmth crept into his veins again. He could not repress it. He had to let it come. The house is a repository of secrets, he excused himself. Then can't mine repose here too?

He went upstairs. He had meant to go to bed – but he picked up the book with the poem, and the words *Love is most nearly itself When here and now cease to matter* seemed to rise to meet him from the print. It was a long poem, that some johnny in the bookshop said Rolls, if he were interested in new poetry, ought to read. Rolls had been turning over several books of poems. 'If you are interested, sir—' 'I am interested in nothing, nothing that happens outside,' Rolls should have said, but instead, in some confusion, he had bought the poem.

Upstairs, on the first-floor landing, is the room that belongs to Griselda, Rolls's mother. Griselda is spoiled; it is a beautiful room with a Morris paper and Morris curtains and colours of blue and peacock-blue and brown and wallflower-brown. Next to it, now inhabited by Rolls himself, is the Eye's, his father's, dressing-room. It communicates with Griselda's by an inner door: Griselda is spoiled but she is always under the Eye.

Next again, past the bathroom, is the room that is Selina's, Rolls's eldest sister. Her room is like her: it is white, it is blue, it is prim; it is full of a clutter of things, but the effect of it is chilly and strangely empty. The stairs lead up and the stairs lead down. After the first floor they lose a little of their spaciousness; after the second floor they narrow and go back to the oilcloth they started with below.

On the second floor back are the nurseries; the windows are level with the top branches of the plane-tree. In the day nursery the nursery furniture is still there, all the fittings: window-bars; the high fender; the rockinghorse whose tail comes out, so that buttons and beads put down it long ago still rattle when it is rocked. Empty nurseries should be forlorn; these are not. They have a definite sense of an inner cheerful life of their own like the sound of the sea, once known to the shell.

The night nursery has been converted into a bedroom: the old nursery furniture is there too – the white-painted chest of drawers, the white-painted bed only wide enough to hold a very slender person, and the nursery curtains of fiddling mice on a pale blue ground. Are they mice? They are so faded they are difficult to see, but Rolls thought that he remembered that they were mice. The carpet is there, blue again and very pale and worn, and on its border skip a frieze of girls and boys perpetually coming out to play in old-time scoop bonnets and old-time hats. Someone has tried to turn the room into a bedroom. There are rugs put down on the carpet, newer rugs, and the dressing-table has been looped into skirts, white muslin ones tied with ribbons that are faded and frayed. There are still brushes on the dressing-table and a pincushion and a little china tray of pins; there is another ribbon, a brown hair-ribbon split into fragments, hanging over the glass. The nursery rocking chair has been painted white and given a clover-pink cushion; there is another little straight-backed chair of the kind that holds clothes folded for the night. There is a bookshelf with two rows of books; children's below; above, an anthology, a little set of classics bound in blue and gold, novels, a *Life of Mozart* and *The Beginner's Book of Stars*. On the shelf there is also a writing case, and if it were opened – and Rolls opened it – there is still a piece of blotting paper that still bears the upside-down imprint of a letter. It begins: *Dear Pelham, As I have decided it is better for me to go away* . . . Rolls did not read it. He knew it.

In the cupboard, if it were opened, are still clothes, folded on the shelves or hanging, their sleeves limp and their skirts wide, from their hooks. On the shelf is a muff with a fox-head that seems to stare; if it is stroked, the hairs fly up from the moths. There is a beaver hat beside it, brown with a brown velvet ribbon and a knot of green feathers: there is moth in that too. By it stands a parasol with the silk cracked from its spokes and the cord and tassel, as good as new, hanging down.

'What shall I do with Miss Lark's things?' asks Agnes, the maid.

'Leave them alone,' says Selina. 'Leave them alone as they are.'

'Excuse me, Miss Selina,' says Proutie, 'is there any news of Miss Lark?'

'None whatever, Proutie. None.'

Mrs Crabbe went up and dusted the top rooms once a week. No one else went into them until Rolls came back to the house. Rolls did not go into the room last night; he did not need to go. He knew it all by heart. He knew the bed and the chairs, the dressing-table and its muslin skirts; the beaver hat; the sense of stillness; the apartness of the young girl's room. He did not go into it. He stayed on the landing reading that poem.

The two flights of stairs, one going up, the other going down, give on the first-floor landing that is wide enough to make a sitting-room. It has an alcove with a window that looks down on the Place, with a window-seat, and by it a table and chairs and a writing desk. The sound of the traffic in the Park Road comes in; and every minute and again, the whole house vibrates slightly as the trains pass underground. The church clock strikes and the clocks follow after it, the clocks outside and the clocks all over the house, and then settle again to their tickings. Every door that opens can be heard on the landing, and every door that shuts; there are rattlings and scrapings when the range is made up. Everything can be heard on the landing.

When Rolls had read the poem he left it open on the book-case and sat down in the armchair and listened until he fell asleep.

'Don't disturb me.' He was always saying that these days to Proutie. 'Don't disturb me,' said the old man, 'I don't want to be disturbed,' and he pushed back in his mind that date that the objectionable Mr Willoughby had mentioned, the fifteenth of December.

There was no one to disturb him. Mrs Crabbe had been gone for hours, and Proutie was out. Three nights a week Proutie was a special constable. Now it was Proutie who had the uniform, Proutie whose comings and goings must be obeyed, Proutie who was of use.

But the bitterness had gone from that. Rolls did not care now. He was in retirement, he had been retired – hung, so the papers said, in his own red tape. He had ceased to care. There was a portrait of him and five other generals of his own day and kind, published in an illustrated paper with six German generals on the opposite page. The comparison was not kind. 'My photograph was taken in nineteen eleven when photographs did look wooden. The Germans were taken to-day.' That was all Rolls had said in his defence; now he would not have even said that: he did not care. 'Don't disturb me,' said Rolls. 'I don't want to be disturbed.'

He thought or dreamed that he was in the drawing-room.

There is a smell of lime-flowers: that means that it is summer. The crystal in the chandelier gives out a chime: that means that somebody is singing, but it is not the somebody that Rolls wanted to hear. Rolls scowled and moved restlessly in his chair. Somebody is singing a hymn. That was not what he intended, but often he is taken on currents like this and not consulted. Dammit! said Rolls. Damnation! Holy Paul! But the someone continues to sing the hymn.

Who is it? His mother? No. She is dead before he ever hears her sing. Selina? It does not seem to be Selina. A governess? Perhaps, but whoever it is she wears a flower in her dress.

'What is its name?'

'"Fight the good fight, with all thy might".'

'No, not the hymn. The flower.'

'It has an easy and a difficult name, but that is too hard for you. I will tell you the easy name.'

'No, I want the difficult name.'

'It is too hard for you.'

'I want it. I want it. Tell it to me.'

She tells it.

Rolls could not remember it. He could remember only the tiny purple fragrant flowers in her dress and that nostalgia stirred in him again, a nostalgia that was as foreign to him, or as forgotten, as the creeping warmth that visited his veins . . . I can't remember the name, but it is somewhere . . . somewhere here in the house.

Then I delighted in difficult things. My mind then was incandescent . . . He is an incandescent little boy. Roly remembers easily, but Rolls had far too long been disciplined and schooled and nowadays his mind refused. He allowed it to refuse, and do as it liked, to shy and to deflect and wander away; to refuse the knowledge that soon, soon it must end and that he must make arrangements to leave the house. Why this passion for exactness? asked Rolls. For labels? I refuse. I refuse to know the date. Let the flower go without a name.

As he said that the singing changed.

For a moment he was still, tense, and then he sank back to listen in his chair.

> Ah – *ahahahahahah* – *ah*
> Ah – *ahahahahahah* – *ah* . . .

It was a different voice, full, strong and young and rich; where the other had attempted the notes, this voice took charge of them, confidently, beautifully.

'There are so many flowers,' said Rolls. 'I didn't have time for flowers but I seem to have learned them lately. Lime-flowers: smilax and lilies and roses: Solomon's lilies: the kitchen chrysan-themums. Roses. Did I say roses? Yellow ones. Why can't I remember that name?'

'Hush,' said the voice. 'Hush. Listen.'

'It wasn't you who wore the flowers,' he persisted. 'Why wasn't it you? You love them. That is what you said.'

'They are the only things that give you comfort without any worry or pain.'

The bitter little speech hurt Rolls. 'I gave you pain, Lark.'

'You gave me pain. But hush,' said the voice. 'Hush. Listen.'

Rolls sank back in the chair and his hand, an old swollen dark-veined, dark-freckled hand, opened on the arm of the chair. A feeling of warmth, of indescribable comfort, filled his body. What was it? It was bliss, and in the quiet, the lateness, in the house, the song went on.

The poem lay open on the bookshelf where Rolls had left it open at that page: –

Home is where one starts from. As we grow older
The world becomes stranger, the pattern more complicated
Of dead and living. Not the intense moment
Isolated, with no before and after,
But a lifetime burning in every moment
And not the lifetime of one man only
But of old stones that cannot be deciphered,

There is a time for the evening under starlight,
A time for the evening under lamplight
(The evening with the photograph album).
Love is most nearly itself
When here and now cease to matter.
Old men ought to be explorers
Here or there does not matter
We must be still and still moving
Into another intensity
For a further union, a deeper communion ...
... In my end is my beginning.

And in the house, the clocks tick; the beams in the night grow hot, grow cold – they creak; a late train runs; a late pedestrian, returning, walks down the Place; a clinker drops in the grate, and a gleam of starlight, coming through the Venetians into the drawing-room, catches the little shepherdess on the clock as she lies dreaming.

Rolls slept in his chair.

MORNING

Before eight o'clock the house is given over to the servants and the children.

Again the past is present.

Roly is being coached by Selina before he has his breakfast and runs off to school, his pre-preparatory school at Dr Butler's in Wiltshire Square. Selina is coaching him in grammar at the table on the landing.

'Take three tenses,' says Selina.

Roly sighs.

'Past, present and future.'

'Must I?'

'Yes you must,' Selina answers him.

Before eight o'clock Proutie, who only came in at four, came down the backstairs and into the kitchen and raked the fire and made it up and opened the boiler to heat the water for Rolls's bath. Then he stroked the cat, opened the door to let it out, and let Mrs Crabbe in.

'Good morning Mrs Crabbe. A quiet night I am glad to say.'

'Good morning Mr Proutie. How wonderfully those chrysanths do smell.'

'I am just taking up a cup of tea to Mr Rolls. I shall make one for us too.'

'I could do with one,' said Mrs Crabbe. 'It pulls your body towards you, don't it? We didn't get much of a night. I tell Alfie we would be far better at home and chance it but there is Em'ly. The shelter every time for her 'e says. No bloomin' risk.'

'No you shouldn't risk it for her,' Proutie agreed, blowing gently on his tea. 'What will you do Mrs Crabbe when we give up the house?'

'Don't name it!' said Mrs Crabbe. 'I just don't take it in. Alfie wants me to take Em'ly to my sister in Cornwall but "Wait till it 'appens" I says.'

While Mrs Crabbe sorted out her brushes and changed her shoes, Proutie laid a tray of tea for Rolls. The distance between butler and charwoman had narrowed; it had almost disappeared. In the old days Proutie had his tea brought to him; he had no occasion to speak to Mrs Crabbe, nor she to him. Now they appreciated one another.

Mrs Crabbe had a song; it could be heard all over the house: –

> Chick chick chick chick chick chick
> Lay a little egg for me.
> Chick chick chick chick chick chick
> I want one for my tea.
> The last I had was Easter
> And now it's half-past three.

Proutie listened to it. He looked at Mrs Crabbe's beret and raincoat and black oilcloth bag hanging on the door and he smiled. Mrs Crabbe was a comfort to him.

When Mrs Sampson is the charwoman she has a bonnet, not a beret; it is a black bonnet with jet trimming and purple strings. Mrs Sampson does the same work as Mrs Crabbe but it is longer and far harder. She has no Hoover nor Bissell carpet-sweeper; no Vim, no Lightning Black; fires are coal fires, there is no electricity; no water is laid on upstairs; there is no bathroom, not for years and years, and no convenient housemaids' cupboard; Mrs Sampson's hands are old and spread, with swollen knuckles and calluses round the nails and cracks at their sides; Mrs Sampson's hands know brooms and dustpans and pump-handles, her elbows are accustomed to the motion of scrubbing and her knees are accustomed to kneeling; she is in fact very accustomed to being down on all fours. Her back knows the strain of coal-scuttles and hot-water pails and she cannot stand up quite straight; whenever she rises into a perpendicular position a spasm of pain twitches her face; she also has varicose veins; she takes a shilling to Mrs Crabbe's half-crown; she has no insurance and old-age pension; she has her meals in the scullery and she calls Mr Athay, the butler, 'sir', and knows he suspects her of stealing the Eye's gin. She does steal the Eye's gin. She knows with an unquenchable sturdy independence that something is due to her out of life. She does not get it so she takes it.

She is Mrs Crabbe's grandmother.

In the garden the house cat tidily raked over the November leaves, hiding the little cocoons of faeces it had made. Under the leaves lies Juno who loves Selina and whom Selina loves. The cat was a common white kitchen cat except that it had one blue eye and one green; like many white cats it was slightly deaf. There is, actually, another cat, Gregory – not after the Pope but because he was the colour of Gregory's powders: he was not as Selina says 'seen to', and he is more out of the house than in it so that the kitchen cat, Mouser, could justly claim to be the house cat.

'I am the house dog.'

Mouser did not hear. He was too busy raking up the leaves.

'I AM THE HOUSE DOG.'

'Well,' said the cat mildly. 'I am the house cat.'

There is sweeping and dusting: brooms and dusters are shaken out of the windows and a housemaid appears with a sacking apron and a pail of water to whiten the front steps. Inside the house, hot water, shaving water and trays of morning tea are taken up. The trays pause outside the dining-room door; Selina first inaugurates morning tea and Proutie as a footman hands out the Apostle spoons. The cans of hot water are heavy; they have brass-bound spouts like port-holes, and they go up as far as the nursery. The Eye has, in his dressing-room, a bath that has to be filled each morning and emptied away; another bath shaped like a saucer is in the nursery. Griselda is up early, she bathes at night; Pelham, when he in his turn inhabits the dressing-room, requires hot water, shaving water and the newspaper in his room: Rollo, on week-end leave from Sandhurst, requires nothing at all: he is still out. His bed is untouched as Agnes turned it down the night before; on his dressing-table in a tooth-glass of water is the one of the two gardenias he did not take to wear. When he comes in he drops the other on the stairs; Lark picks it up and presses it and keeps it.

Proutie came upstairs with Rolls's tea. He knocked at the dressing-room door.

It is half-past eight.

The Eye and Griselda come out of Griselda's room. They have separated while they dressed, now they go down to breakfast together and the Eye unnecessarily guides Griselda with his hand under her elbow.

He is a very large, very well made young man of twenty-nine, with a large clever forehead, pale-brown hair and pale-blue shrewd steady eyes. By the side of his pallor, Griselda glows. Perhaps this is what first attracted him to her, the warmth and colour she has that he lacks. He knows that he needs it. He chose Griselda much as he chose the sapphire blue waistcoat that in its deepness redeems the drab broadcloth of his suit; he chose her as he chose his ruby pin, as he loves rubies, for their fire; but fire can hurt. His eyes follow Griselda; there is no doubt in them, no questioning of his position or hers, but often when Griselda thinks him immersed in something else, his eyes are following her still.

Griselda this morning is seventeen; very young, very eager and singularly unalloyed. She is tall but beside the Eye she seems little; her eyes are dark blue and her hair is chestnut, brilliantly rich and dressed in curls each side of the parting that the Eye looks down on, running broad and white and sensitive from her forehead to the knot that holds her hair on top of her head and from which falls another cascade of curls. That parting is singularly straight, and so is Griselda's nose, and so is the look in her eyes, but the Eye, always bending to look into them from a sentimental angle, has not seen that yet. Griselda is dressed this morning in a wide blue dress, but a much deeper blue than the waistcoat; colours for married women now, however young, are deep or sombre while for girls they are strong and bright. Griselda

27

is no longer only a girl; she is a married woman, fashionably, suitably dressed. The skirt that clogs her movements is fashionably full; the neck is low and the sleeves short: she wears for warmth a little tartan shawl and she has a set of heavy jewellery in gold with a mosaic of blue and red: earrings, bracelet and brooch.

Breakfast is laid on the table in the dining-room where the sun catches the wedding silver, an October sun. There is a vase of Michaelmas daisies on the table. 'Our Michaelmas daisies,' says the Eye. He has a well-developed sense of property. Griselda hesitates and the Eye pulls out her chair at the bottom of the table. 'This is your place, love.'

'Yes John.'

The Eye goes to his, and picks up the paper that is lying by his plate. Griselda looks at him and hesitates again and then lifts up the teapot.

'Do you take sugar John?'

He laughs at her over the paper. 'Don't you think you should remember after all this time? A whole honeymoon, Griselda?'

But she is serious. She flushes. 'I was thinking.'

She imagines he is reading but he is watching her. He would like to know what it is she thinks of. A woman's thoughts are a new idea to the Eye; he had not known they had them, not thoughts such as he suspects Griselda's to be. Sometimes she is with him, but sometimes she is equally absent, strangely she is not there; sometimes she looks at him as if she had never seen him before. If he asked her what she was thinking of, he knows, after six months of engagement and their honeymoon, that he would not succeed in getting an answer. He sighs. He is beginning to realize that not all of Griselda, not the whole, will always belong to him.

Now she turns her face that glows so vividly, so beautifully with life that it catches his breath, towards him. 'Think John! This is the first breakfast!' Her joy is solemn. 'Think. No one has ever eaten breakfast in this house before!'

'Except six servants for three weeks,' says the Eye.

Occasionally the Eye loves Griselda more than he can bear. Then he has to hide himself and be brusque.

'Have we really six servants?'

'Yes, my dear, and your mother chose them, so they are sure to be paragons. They are yours to direct and command.'

'I don't think I am very good at directing and commanding,' says Griselda.

The Eye is reading the paper. She lifts the heavy cover off the dish that is embossed and twined with silver grapes. It is hard to believe that anything as weighty and important-looking is hers. Her nose wrinkles at the steamy smell that comes out under it.

'John?'

'Mmm'm?'

'John, do you *like* haddock for breakfast?'

'No,' says the Eye immediately. 'You must tell Cook.'

Griselda hesitates and looks at him and looks at the haddock. 'John, have you seen Cook?'

'Yes?'

'You tell her,' says Griselda.

The Eye laughs at her but again there is no answering laugh on her face or in her eyes. I have been thinking – seriously.

'This is a very big house for only two people,' says Griselda doubtfully.

'There may not always be only two people, my little dearest.'

She looks at him as she understands his meaning; the colour in her cheeks deepens but still she does not smile.

'What is it, Griselda?'

'That – is part of what I mean,' says Griselda very slowly. 'Part of it. I know I shouldn't say things like this to you John, but it – all this – seems as if it might swallow – people's lives.'

He comes round the table to her at once, dropping his paper on the floor. 'I won't let it swallow you.'

She turns to him and he feels she is fierce in the way she clings to him and looks at him. 'Promise! Promise!'

All at once, for some reason that he prefers not to know, he cannot look back at her. He would rather not look at her and meet her gaze. He holds her in his arms and kisses her and smooths her hair.

'Promise.'

'I promise.'

Perhaps she feels his mood. She asks: 'John, are you laughing?'

'No, I am not laughing,' says the Eye.

'One day,' says Griselda suddenly, 'you won't drop your paper. You will go on reading it. You won't hear.'

He looks at her gravely. 'I think you will have to trust me, Griselda.'

She is disarmed at once. 'Oh John. I do. I do.'

'I want a big house,' says the Eye. 'My ideas, my schemes, are big. Very ambitious and very, very big.'

Griselda is still doubtful. 'Do you mean we shall become – substantial?' she asks. 'I don't know that I shall like that.'

'You will. I shall see to that. I think, my darling, I know you better than you know yourself.'

'Do you?' asks Griselda, but she does not sound convinced.

'How can you? How can you feel what I feel? I feel so – mixed, John.'

'Yes?' encourages the Eye.

'I feel—' But she does not say it. She cannot tell John, who still, besides being her lover, persists in being a stranger, she cannot tell him that sometimes since she was engaged, since she was married, she feels as if she had been put in prison with a life sentence. She says involuntarily, hastily, 'Don't be successful too quickly, will you John!'

He does not answer and she says as if she were discovering something, 'Sometimes John, you remind me a little of my father.' The Eye laughs again but Griselda says thoughtfully, 'I never very much liked my father.'

'You will always like me,' says the Eye quite quietly and confidently. 'Can I read my paper now?'

'Of course. I want you to,' says Griselda. 'I know brides are supposed to mind that but I don't. I mean to read the paper myself every day. I don't see why a woman should not be the equal of men in that. I want us to be well informed – about everything, John. All sorts of things. I don't see why we should shut ourselves away in our own affairs, behind our walls, just because we have a house and a – you said it first John – a family. I want to keep in touch with the world,' says Griselda looking far, far into a width of distance. 'I want to learn. I consider I am just at the beginning of my education John. I mean to go on learning. And touching and tasting and seeing and wondering until I die, and I mean to be a very old lady I warn you. I want to learn languages and then visit the countries and see if I can talk to the people and understand them. I want every day and every year to enlarge my mind and try and understand a little more. I could be your equal in that couldn't I John? That wouldn't be – presumptuous? Both of us, together, exploring all these things!'

She recalls her eyes from that distance and seeks the Eye's face but she can only see the top of his well-brushed pale-brown head bent into the newspaper. Her eyes widen. Then they harden.

'Of course,' says Griselda after a minute, 'to begin with there ought to be two papers.'

It is eight o'clock.

Before the grown-ups are awake the children are out of bed.

They step into a secret servant-ridden world that their elders do not have a chance to see. Servitude, in most people, induces a second face; Mrs Proutie, Agnes, Athay, Slater, Mrs Sampson, even Proutie, have it. The servants have their world; the children have theirs; they impinge on one another and are commonly impinged on by authority. Authority again has a world to itself, separated into the orbits of men and women. These are worlds within a world, circling round one another and round the suns of religion, custom, money, love – inhabiting the universe that is a house.

Roly, jumping down the stairs, jumps into Mrs Sampson, sweeping on the landing. 'Good morning Mrs Sampson. How are your veins?'

Mrs Sampson wipes her nose on the back of her hand and says her veins are bad.

'And your sister's kidneys?' Roly is just putting off time and he knows it. Unfortunately Mrs Sampson knows it too.

'Poorly thank you, Master Roly,' says Mrs Sampson. 'Now you must get out of my way and get on yours. It is time for your lessings.'

Roly goes slowly towards the table.

> *Chick chick chick chick chick chick*
> *Lay a little egg for me.*

Mrs Crabbe wheeled the Hoover briskly out of the drawing-room and plugged it into the study wall, shaking the rugs and clearing away Rolls's litter before she started on the carpet.

Mrs Sampson stiffly stands up. For a moment she stays with one hand pressed to her back and her face twisted, until the spasm that she expects and receives has passed. Then with a sigh of which she is not aware, she gathers up her brush and dustpan full of carpet fluff and goes downstairs.

What a great deal of dirt and dust must be taken out of this house and put into the dustbin, thinks little Roly at the table. And taken out of the dustbin, he goes on, and put into the dust-cart and carted away all over London.

'Are we only dust when we die?' he asks suddenly.

'Certainly not,' says Selina. 'We are angels.'

'Or devils,' says Roly with a chuckle.

Ever since Roly was born and Griselda died Selina has been shaping him, patiently, quite gently on the whole, but quite implacably to her will, but he still says things like this. 'That is nothing to laugh about,' says Selina. 'It is serious.' Roly yawns.

Selina is very like the Eye; she is a large well-made young woman with pale colouring and a steady clever face. Like the Eye she is possessive but where the Eye is tempered with wisdom and genuine kindness, Selina is not. Roly is like Griselda, with her warm skin and brilliant eyes and hair, but he has not the straightness of Griselda's nose nor of Griselda's eyes. Roly gives in.

'When I grow up,' says Roly, 'I am going to be a tailor like Mr Cheep. He says I have the finest chest in London. I like Mr Cheep.'

'You will go into the Army like Uncle Bunny,' says Selina. Uncle Bunny is Roly's godfather, an exalted godfather.

'No I won't,' says Roly. 'Soldiers get killed. And they have to kill other people. I shan't like that.'

'The killing is only a small part.'

'What else is there?'

'Brains! Strategy!' cries Selina with shining eyes.

Roly looks at her. He does not ask her why she is not a soldier because he knows that girls are never anything, but he wishes for a moment that he had been born a girl. This is the last time he ever wishes that; he quickly sets into the fact of being a boy. There is very little that is feminine in Rollo or in Rolls. Selina does with him all that she hopes and wants but in some curious way he still eludes her; he prefers the Eye to her for instance, and yet the Eye can hardly bear to notice him though he fulfils punctiliously all that he did with the other children; Roly still persists in liking dirt and marbles and vulgar sweets and he still makes vulgar friends like Mr Cheep. He is still, mysteriously, himself.

'Sit *up* Roly.'

'Why, as soon as I am told to sit *down*, am I told to sit *up*?'

'Take three tenses.'

Roly sighs.

'Past, present and future.'

'Must I?'

'Yes, you must,' says Selina. 'Even a little boy like you has a past, a present and a future. You were a baby, you are a boy, you will be a man.'

'And then dust,' says Roly. 'But I am always here, Lena. Like they say at school "Present." I am always present so why not only one?'

Selina is called Lena when she is a little girl. She is an extremely controlled little girl, very good and precocious. She is the pride and joy of her nurse and she wants, violently, to be the pride and joy of her mother, but Griselda in some way or another seems always to escape from her. Griselda is not unkind, never neglectful, but 'Go to nurse,' 'It is time for you to go upstairs now,' sounds like a reprieve on Griselda's lips. The boys are early sent to school but Lena is a little girl. She should stay at home, be with her mother. 'Presently,' 'By and by,' says Griselda.

'You must learn to read, you little dunce,' she says when Selina is five.

'And you are going to teach me?' Lena is joyous. She knows she is anything but a little dunce.

'We will ask Papa to get a governess for you.'

Griselda has asked Papa very frequently why Lena, and Elizabeth too in her turn, should not also go to school. 'Perhaps even one day to college. There is talk of a woman's college at Oxford now.'

'These are – rather unusual ideas for girls, my dearest.'

'Why?' asks Griselda. 'They are the same ideas as you had for the boys.'

'Well—' says the Eye, but he has the wisdom, as he is in a hurry to go out, not to engage on that point. He says instead, 'You must remember we have six sons to educate.'

'We should be fair. Lena has as good and quick a brain as any of the boys. Better than most of them.'

'I am sure she has, but it won't be necessary for her to exploit it in the same way.'

'It is given her to use.'

'So she shall – up to a point. She shall have a governess. We get an excellent superior person for – say – twenty pounds a year.'

'And meanwhile the boys – even James who is so stupid?'

'James may have to support a family when he is grown up. Lena will not. Don't frown Griselda. That is indisputable.'

'Yes John,' says Griselda. 'It is indisputable but it is not the whole dispute.'

'My dear, surely you want our sons – even James – to be brought up as gentlemen? He is not the milkman's son.'

It is odd that the Eye should choose that for his point. When Verity is thirteen the question of his senior school arises. Grizel is asked where he will go.

'We had hoped he might follow Pax to Eton,' says Grizel, 'but I doubt now if he has the brains to get in. Isn't it splendid,' says Grizel, 'Jopling's son has just passed in there. He is such a brilliant boy and of course now Eton is for scholars. Verity will get a grammar school and perhaps two or three years in an exchange to Canada or Australia and of course some time in Italy. He will have estates to manage so they think agriculture—'

'Who is Jopling, Grizel?'

'Our milkman,' says Grizel.

Meanwhile the Eye rules that a governess is sufficient for Lena.

She is too proud to love her governess as she was too proud to love her nurse. Whom can she love? A pet? Pets are not allowed. Once she finds a dead mouse on the stairs and keeps it for three days, until her nurse, horrified, makes her throw it away. When she is older she loves Roly, Rollo, but this love becomes implicated and mixed with such possessiveness and jealousy that Rollo will not have it and Selina is left bitterly alone. It is then that she buys Juno.

Juno is a pug, stuffed to repletion with a gold plush coat and a tail like a curl of vaseline and warm wallflower markings in her creases and on her ears. 'She couldn't love it more if it was human,' the servants say. 'It might be human the way she goes on.' They are wrong. It is not Selina who is making Juno into a human – but Juno, Selina.

There is a noise like a chirping of sparrows all over the house. It is the happiest children. It is the twins.

'Freddie. Elizabeth. Come and get dressed.'

'No,' says Elizabeth. 'I am going in to Mamma.'

No other child is allowed to go in to Mamma. Griselda is not just. She does not attempt to be just. When she loves, she shows it, and she cannot forget when she is hurt. Pelham, John Robert, Lionel, James, Selwyn and Selina, even Freddie, had big heads like the Eye's; they tore and hurt Griselda hideously when they were born and the horror of that for her is inevitably attached to them. She tries to forget it, but she cannot; nor can she forget that it was the Eye who inflicted them on her. Inflicted? Yes. Left to myself, says Griselda, would I have chosen to have children? Yes. One. Possibly two . . . but the Eye has big ideas. 'Nine is my lucky number,' says the Eye. In all her feelings for him she remembers that.

Elizabeth, her eighth child, slipped easily into the world half an hour after Freddie, and she was a tiny baby with a small round firm head. 'A delicate child,' they told Griselda. 'That is the way with twins.' 'Not a fine child like the others,' said Nurse. 'Fine. Much finer,' said Griselda fiercely. 'Fine in my way, not in yours.'

Elizabeth is a forerunner of Roly. The other children are all replicas of the Eye, with his pale skin and pale blue eyes and mouse-brown hair. Elizabeth has chestnut hair and sparkling daring dark-blue eyes.

'You are not just,' says the Eye to Griselda; the boys say it too; Lena is rude about it; Nurse complains. 'You spoil Elizabeth,' says Nurse.

I don't care. I don't want to be just, says Griselda silently but she tries to make herself listen and for a day or two sends Elizabeth back to the nursery.

Now and again, through the house, up the stairs, there flies a little boy who seems to belong to nobody; a little interloper. He is small and thin and dark-skinned and he is dressed in a foreign-looking dark-blue sailor suit, and black stockings and shoes. The shoes kick in the air with ecstasy and his eyes are always shut with bliss. He never walks. He always flies. Slowly he flies out of sight. Every now and again he comes again.

The children play with the stones when they have prunes for lunch: —

> *Soldier brave,*
> *Sailor true,*
> *Lawyer grave,*
> *Doctor blue.*

'A blue doctor?' asks Elizabeth. 'But Dr Flower is pink.'

> *Portly rector,*
> *Curate pale . . .*

'When I marry the curate I am going to be married by the Bishop,' says Lena. 'And the church shall be decorated in lilies and smilax – no, roses and smilax – no, lilies, roses *and* smilax, and I shall have eight bridesmaids dressed in purest white—'

'Suppose he, or nobody, asks you?' tease the boys.

'I shall give them no peace till they do,' says Lena.

When Roly goes to school and is called Rollo the nursery is empty. No one knows why the sound of the sea, once known to the shell, should still be there, but no one can deny that it is.

As soon as Lark follows Selina over the threshold of the nursery she is in touch with the other children. To begin with, though she has nothing to do with them, as Selina is always reminding her, she inherits their things: she sleeps in their bed, her clothes are, some of them, their clothes, and she keeps her clothes in their cupboards; she eats off their old china with their nursery spoons and forks; she plays with the rocking horse and Lena's old doll's tea-set; she reads the books that have their names on the flyleaves: *Selwyn. A happy Christmas from Aunt Nellie. Dec. 1853. Rollo from his Father on his eighth birthday. 1871.*

Lark is a lonely child. There is no one to notice her in the house; the Eye, who brought her there, is too busy and too sad. Selina shuts her away at the top of the house. Lark's mind in its loneliness and unhappiness fastens on these children and most of all, perhaps because he is next in age to her, perhaps because he is so important to Selina who dominates her, and to whom she is so unimportant, Lark fastens upon Roly. She takes Roly for a friend and a brother and when she plays at weddings she takes him for a husband; like Lena, like the other children, she quite often plays at weddings. 'I Roly Dane, take thee Lark, for my wedding wife and we shall have six children and a million pounds a year.'

Lark is wrong in one thing. She is not unimportant to Selina.

It begins early one late December morning at the end of eighteen seventy-nine. The weather, all the week before it, had been unusually wild and there was talk of ships lost at sea, of great trees blown down and in the North of havoc over huge districts and towns. The weather seemed to rise in a crescendo.

Selina is heavily asleep when Athay wakes her, knocking and knocking at her door. 'Miss Lena. Miss Selina. Will you get up miss. The master has come. Will you come down to the study at once.'

'Father?' cries Selina. 'But he is in Edinburgh!'

'He is here. In the study miss.'

'Athay. Has anything happened?'

A pause. 'He asks you to come down miss,' says Athay.

Selina does not wait to put up her hair. She comes with a long plait hanging down her back to the end of her shawl. Her forehead with her hair strained back looks clever and indomitable and obstinate as she confronts the Eye. She has a dressing gown of Indian silk with a design of brown swans under Persian trees.

Athay has lit the fire but it is still new enough to crackle and flare with its paper and send out a cold blue smoke; the coals are still untouched and the room has no warmth in it. The Eye has not taken off his travelling coat, a great strapped coat with a cape lined with plaid. His face looks tired and grey and very grave and sad. On the hearthrug stands a little girl well wrapped-up and dressed in mourning.

'A child!' cries Selina in the doorway. There is nothing but dismay in her voice. She does not like children. She loved Roly but not because he was a child but because he would presently grow into the man she wanted him to be. She likes him better now he is at school, she will like him more when he is at Sandhurst and grown up. She does not go if she can help it into the nurseries of her friends, nor glance into perambulators, nor watch the nun on her slow progression to the Park with all her orphans on their reins. 'I could have had children I suppose,' says Selina but she has no desire that is at all alive or active to have them. She is perhaps too interested in herself to want to give more than a very little of that interest away; what she gives, she gives to Rollo, but then of course she looks on Rollo as a projection of herself. Then with the Eye this child appears. In that instant Selina knows it is to be no slight appearance. She stiffens. She has an immediate sense of trouble and threat. 'A child!'

'Lark, this is Selina.'

'How do you do,' says Lark politely. Her voice is almost extinct with tiredness. Lark is seven and she is at the moment filled with one overwhelming need, a body that needs to be lain down somewhere to sleep and sleep and sleep. The Eye has tried to comfort her but he continually asks her questions: 'Are you crying?' 'Would you like some milk?' 'Some soup?' 'A chocolate?' 'You will tell me if you want anything won't you?' 'Are you warm enough?' To all of them Lark answered politely but she was growing desperate. The Eye talked of Selina. 'When we get to Selina she will look after you.' 'Selina will put you to bed.' Now her longing flows out like a wave to Selina and like a wave it recoils back again on herself. She fixes her eyes, firmly, to look firmly at the end of Selina's plait to prevent them filling with tears. Grown-up people, especially men, she thinks do not say what is true, but what they hope is true. She can see at once there is no help for her in Selina.

'Who is she?' asks Selina.

'Her name is Lark Ingoldsby.'

'Ingoldsby? Like the Legends?'

'Please don't make jokes, Selina.' There is so much pain in the Eye's voice that Selina stops, trembling.

'What is it, Father?'

'Her father and – mother were killed in the Tay Bridge disaster, the night before last.'

Selina's quick mind is caught at once by that infinitesimal pause in his voice before he said 'mother'. She has not really heard the rest. She says mechanically, 'Tay Bridge?'

'It will be in the morning papers. It was a dreadful night,' he goes on with an effort. 'Violent and wild. They think – the covered way of the bridge offered – too much – resistance to the wind. The people waiting in the station saw – the lighted train go into the bridge – then there was darkness.'

'It – never came out?'

'It never came out. The bridge was gone.' The Eye turns away from her to the mantelpiece and covers his eyes with his hand.

Lark hears it being said over her head. She has heard it being said over her head over and over again in the last twenty-four hours. She has taken her eyes away from Selina's plait and is looking at the hearthrug because tears of themselves have begun again to slide down her nose, but her black hair falls each side of her neck and hides her face and nobody can see. She is indeed as black as a little crow. The Eye told the manageress of the hotel to get her into mourning and she is black from head to foot and her hat which she has taken off and put into a chair is heavily trimmed with crape. She feels bowed down with blackness and the tears run down the side of her nose where she has hidden her face. The little nape of her neck gleams like the marble Caesar in the room.

'Then all the people Father?'

'No one was saved.'

He takes down his hand. 'You will have to know,' he says in a flat weary voice, 'that her father and – mother were singers, opera singers. She – had a beautiful voice. That is why I went North, to hear her sing.'

'*Father!*'

'Yes,' says the Eye without the least emotion in his voice. 'They had taken an engagement in pantomime in Stirling for Christmas week. Dundee the week after.'

'In *pantomime?*'

'Yes,' says the Eye again. 'I had business in Dundee so I went on by the morning train and took Lark with me.'

'Else—'

'Else I should have been with the company in that train,' says the Eye plainly, 'and so would she.'

Lark has ceased to hear what they say. Their voices sound and resound over her head as the black wooliness of the hearthrug, yes it is black too, seems to rise up in front of her eyes into peculiar hills and fall away again; she is now not even conscious of being tired; only her eyes smart and the smell of the new clothes is overpowering, stuffy in her nostrils.

'I went down by chaise but there was nothing –' Again he turns away and Selina waits and does not prompt him. 'Nothing to be done. So I brought Lark here.'

'Why?'

'She has no one. No relations.'

'I thought people of that sort teemed with relations.' He does not answer, only looks at her gravely, but Selina is intrepid. 'There is an orphanage over the way.'

'She is to live here always.'

Selina does not answer. She has grown very white and faces the Eye as he faces her.

'Her past is over, Lena. It is nothing to do with you.'

'Is that all you can tell me, Father?'

'That is all I intend to tell you.'

The clock ticks. A coal drops in the grate where the fire is warm now. The black hillocks rise and tumble in front of Lark.

'Her mother is dead, Lena.'

'So is mine.'

At that moment Lark falls on the hearthrug. The Eye picks her up and she lies across his arm, her small white face drowned in her hair, meshes of hair caught across his chest and hand. 'This is my house,' says the Eye sternly over Lark's head. 'My house, though I have let you give orders in it. It is my house and I intend to be obeyed. Lark is to come here and live here as your sister. Do you understand?'

'Yes Father.' She looks at Lark in his arms where she used to lie, and her lips tighten.

'You are to write and tell Pelham and the boys and Rollo.'

44

'Yes Father.'

'Then what is that expression on your face?'

'Nothing Father.'

'Answer me.'

'I was thinking,' and she says: 'You told me to answer you. I was thinking, sisters are born, not made. I don't think you can expect, Father, that we shall feel her to be a sister.'

Selina is quite right.

It is another day, about five years later on – a June morning. Selina is giving her orders.

She is dressed to go out and as she crosses the drawing-room to the desk, her dress trails fashionably after her along the carpet; its dark green fullness is looped and gathered behind; the bodice is tight-fitting with tight-fitting sleeves buttoned to the elbows with tiny gilt buttons; her gloves are dark green and so is her jacket that is trimmed with sable: they lie on the sofa. Her hat has a fall of feathers, brilliant green and russet, and her hair is dressed high showing her ears; it gives her a commanding look; in fact it and the feathers make her look not unlike a general setting out to review his troops. Selina is reviewing her day. The table is covered with memorandum pads and there is an engagement pad standing on the desk with spaces closely filled in. It is headed *The second of June, eighteen eighty-five*. It is Selina's thirty-fifth birthday.

In the years since Griselda died, twenty-two years ago, there has hardly been a blank hour for Selina; though she still grieves for Griselda, free of her chain of jealousy, she has been able to organize her life so that it has passed smoothly and efficiently and busily; so busily that she has hardly had time to know that it has passed; it has gone almost unfelt. She has kept house for the Eye since she was sixteen with great authority and she is far more efficient than Griselda, though the house is strangely not as comfortable. The Eye shuts himself away in the study. Pelham, and Rollo when he is home on leave, are almost always out.

Beyond the table Mrs Proutie is waiting. She is still the cook. Most of the servants in the house are annuals, a few are perennials: Mrs Sampson, Mrs Crabbe, Agnes, Athay, Slater, Proutie and Mrs Proutie are the perennials. Mrs Proutie is a formidable woman with a mighty bust and her hair is dressed as high as Selina's own and caught up with combs. She wears a print dress, pink, and an immense rustling starched apron. She smells always of flour and cabbage and a little of the comfortable smell of singed linen, from the warmth of that apron as it bends over the fire, and a little of sweat. She cannot altogether imbue Griselda with awe, Griselda has a way of escaping, but she stands no nonsense from Selina.

'You understand about the soubise, don't you Mrs Proutie?' says Selina.

'I should 'ope so,' says Mrs Proutie. They are discussing Selina's birthday dinner. 'And then there will be a nice saddle of mutting to follow. You can leave *that* to me. And we will end with those nice butting mushrooms in cream on toast with the little bacon rolls.'

There is perpetually, in the house, a plethora of food. The butcher, the baker, the fishmonger, the poulterer, the grocer and the greengrocer all call for orders and the orders are substantial, especially for the butcher.

Now in the meat cage in the larder were only the crops, the ration for Proutie and Rolls, for half a week. It looked strangely empty. It is accustomed to hold, in Mrs Proutie's time, for one day, perhaps a dozen sausages on a plate; a leg of mutton; four pounds of fillet of steak and a chicken with its head and feet and liver tidily arranged beside it. There is also a cut ham, and a side of bacon. Below on a stone slab under the north window are perhaps a few pounds of turbot or fillets of sole; four cod steaks for the kitchen; some kippers for breakfast; a few dozen whiskery shrimps in a bowl; and the cats' fish in a saucer. There are other bowls: a bowl of country eggs sent specially by carrier; butter, with the wooden shaping slats beside it; fruit; stewed fruit cooling; cream; milk in bowls that are glazed brown outside and cream-glazed in. There is a Stilton covered in a corner, and the remains of an open apricot tart and half a custard. There is a great crock for bread, and a vegetable rack, and lemons, and parsley in a jug and a bouquet of herbs and, hanging from the ceiling, strings of onions. Across the passage is the store-room to which Griselda is always losing the key; from its closed door a good smell comes out of coffee and brown sugar and vinegar. It has shelves of tins and jars and packets. A stair leads down to the cellar but Griselda does not have the key of that: Athay has it, and Slater, and of course Mrs Proutie; the Eye has a commendable little store of wine.

Everyone in the house has a favourite dish and Mrs Proutie in however bad a temper always remembers them on birthdays. For the Eye it never changes: it is always roast beef and Yorkshire pudding but it has to be cooked on a spit as only Mrs Proutie can cook it; for Pelham it is jugged hare and sometimes mushrooms; for Roly pink meringues with raspberry jam inside; for Selina it may be some newfangled thing that she has set her heart on – if Mrs Proutie allows it. She does not like newfangled things.

'Now what about the sweet?' she says and fixes her eye on Selina. Selina indomitably fixes her eye on Mrs Proutie.

'I want something rather special,' begins Selina and the battle is on.

'*If* it is to be those jelly nests in angelica seaweed, I am not making them, Miss Lena, nor a fool of meself on a dinner party night.'

'But—'

'What about a trifle?' Mrs Proutie mows her down.

'We always have a trifle.'

'An' why? You ast for something special and special you know very well that trifle is Miss Lena. It is me grandmother's grandmother's recipe and you don't get a trifle like it in any other 'ouse that I do know. People know a good thing when they taste it, make no mistake about that. They don't like your narsty foreign made-up messes.'

'Very well then,' says Selina. 'Trifle.'

'Not if you say it like that Miss Lena, birthday or no birthday.'

'Oh, Mrs Proutie. I didn't mean—' says Selina hastily. She knows what will happen if Mrs Proutie should be in a temper that night.

'Miss Lena I have known you since the day you was born and I know what is in your mind. The recipe is me grandmother's grandmother's and I shall 'and it on, but I am not making it anywhere where it isn't appreciatit and so I tell you flat, no matter 'ow old you are.'

Selina has to spend ten of her precious minutes to placate her. 'I am sure everything will be *delightful*,' she says silkily, peeping at her watch that is pinned on her bodice. She has arranged that, while she talks to Mrs Proutie, the Parish worker who is coming to see her should wait ready in the dining-room. She has a few minutes to see her in before she need start for the committee meeting at ten o'clock. 'Do you get good news of little Harry?' she asks peeping at the watch.

Little Harry is Proutie at the convent orphanage over the way, but Mrs Proutie has something more to say.

'I shall be out for lunch and tea,' says Selina. 'Professor Freyburg is coming at five; he may want tea. I shall see him when I come in. I think that is all, Mrs Proutie.' But Mrs Proutie has something to say.

'Yes?' says Selina reluctantly.

'Miss Lena, it is not my affair but 'aven't you any orders for Miss Lark?'

'For Lark?'

'Yes Miss Lena. I must say the child doesn't look cared for at all. Agnes 'asn't time to see her, besides it isn't reely 'er work. She did ought to 'ave a governess or be sent to school.'

'Father won't send her to school.'

'Well I don't know about that,' says Mrs Proutie, 'but I do know that she is in your charge and the way she looks doesn't reflect no credit on you Miss Lena. She doesn't look like a lady's child at all.'

She isn't a lady's child, Selina almost said, but she checked it just in time. 'Send for her then,' she said. 'But I have to see Miss Dunn.'

Lark appears. She is looking pale and her hair is unkempt and her dress is stained and rubbed at the elbows. She certainly does not reflect, like the rest of the house, Selina's efficient shining care. 'Everythings flourish under your touch.' That was what that Baron, that friend of the Eye's, had said. It was particularly gratifying coming from a Baron. 'Everythings'! *Everything except humans.* Where did that whisper come from? She is suddenly put in mind of scenes with Roly; with Rollo; of the Eye's absence in the study; and now Lark, pale and shabby, stands silently, fearfully, in front of the desk. Like her great-niece Grizel, Selina is a very positive person, firm and decided, and does not admit of doubts in her mind. Then how did this doubt come in? It is not a doubt. It is an omission. There is, is there, something *lacking* in Selina? Unlike her great-niece she never finds it out.

She turns to Lark: on Lark.

'You haven't brushed your hair.'

'No,' Lark agrees politely.

'Why not? You have a hairbrush.' She does not wait for an answer. 'Put on a clean dress. I won't have you going about like this.'

'I haven't a clean dress. This is my winter one. The other is too thin.'

'You can put on a jacket. What are you going to do to-day?'

'What?' asks Lark in alarm.

'Surely you must know what you have to do?'

'Oh,' says Lark in relief. 'Nothing.'

'Nothing?'

'Nothing.'

The content in Lark's voice arrests Selina. 'Do you *like* to have nothing to do the whole day?'

'I do things. I read – and I go out in the garden.'

'But nothing organized?' says Selina. 'You must have lessons. Why, you are quite old. You must have your day filled up.'

'Then what time would I have for – for—'

'For what?'

'For myself.'

'For yourself? What an odd idea! Don't you want to get on, to learn lessons? Isn't there anything you want to learn?' Selina is interested in spite of herself.

'I used to have music.' Lark does not often mention to Selina what she used or used not to have. 'I should like to learn music again.'

'Music lessons are expensive.'

'You have plenty of money.'

Selina looks across the desk at Lark. She sees that Lark is getting tall and slim; she sees the black hair complained about lying like a web on Lark's shoulders and she sees suddenly that the pale serene small face has contours that are unexpectedly beautiful; Lark is looking down and her eyelashes are long and black and curling, but when she makes her answers she lifts her eyes and then there is a flash of brilliant violet blue. Selina sees all at once, that morning, that moment, that Lark is an unusually beautiful child and she is as outraged as if a cuckoo had put an egg in her nest. She says with a surge of extraordinary unkindness: 'You don't understand your position, Lark. You are a penniless orphan. You are very lucky to have been given anything at all. You might have been left to beg in the streets. Your father and mother were paupers.'

'They were not. They were singers.'

'They didn't leave you a penny. You might have starved but for Father. You might have had to be in an orphanage, like the convent, like little Harry Proutie.'

'He seems to be quite a happy child,' says Lark judiciously.

'How dare you!' cries Selina. 'He is not nearly as happy and as lucky as you ought to be without asking for expensive lessons.'

'I didn't ask,' says Lark. 'You asked me. I will ask the Eye,' she says with sudden spirit.

'You will call him Mr Dane.' Lark looks back steadily and Selina cries: 'He spoils you. That is the trouble. He gives in to you.'

'He forgets all about me,' says Lark in a low voice.

Slater comes in. 'Miss Dunn is here.'

'Ask her to come in,' says Selina. 'Lark, I haven't time to go into all this now, but there will have to be an alteration in your manners and behaviour. Ask Agnes to brush your hair and I shall see she takes you for a walk. When you come in, you can write me an essay on – on—' says Selina looking round. She catches sight of a mission postcard on her desk. 'On "Africa. I should like to visit it and why."'

'But I shouldn't like to visit Africa,' says Lark politely, and she says hastily, 'May I write one on Italy? It says in the book *"There was a smell of warm apricots and I looked out of the catacomb, through the grating, and there were thousands of freesias that smelt like apricots in the hot sun."* I shall visit Italy when I am grown up.'

'You will have to earn your living when you are grown up. You won't have time to visit anywhere,' says Selina crushingly.

'No, I shall marry,' says Lark.

Slater opens the door and Miss Dunn comes in. She is an elderly single woman who knew Griselda; Selina calls her an old maid and, because she is poor and insignificant, she allows her to come out early on any Parish errand. To-day she has come about the Parish magazine: she has the proofs in her bag.

'Good morning Selina. Good morning Lark dear child.'

Selina already has a peremptory hand out for the proofs but Miss Dunn goes on. 'What a beautiful beautiful day.'

Selina does not answer. She has taken the proofs.

'It is all blue and sun,' says Lark.

'And what are you going to do in it?' asks Miss Dunn.

'I shall be in the garden,' says Lark.

'Yes, you should, dear child. You should go out early on a morning like this. Dear me, I could smell the lime-flowers as I came along.'

'What is it you wanted me to see?' asks Selina. 'I have a meeting at ten.'

'They are not quite right,' says Miss Dunn as she turns over the proofs and her beatific expression fades and her face looks like a worried wrinkled walnut. 'There is a little matter—' In her shabby cotton mended glove she turns the pages. 'Oh dear! Now I have dropped it. I had better take off my glove.'

'What number is it?' says Selina impatiently.

'Wait. Now. There it is.' She has taken off her glove. Really, what a comedy of a glove – and she peers round Selina's arm. 'There, dear, do you see? If Hitchcock's advertisement goes under Gryce's he will be offended but Gryce gave twenty *pounds* to the Organ Fund. Do you see *how* difficult it is?'

'It isn't difficult,' says Selina taking a pencil. 'Put it like this, and this.' The pencil makes smooth lines and arrows on the paper. 'That paragraph moved up here. Now the two advertisements are parallel and neither of them can grumble. It is quite simple.'

'Yes,' says Miss Dunn, 'now I see you do it. You are a clever girl, Selina,' she says thoughtfully as Selina briskly rolls up the proofs and gives them back to her. 'What a pity it is,' says Miss Dunn, 'that you can't do something big.'

'Big?' asks Selina in surprise.

'Yes. You are so capable,' says Miss Dunn. 'You have such a good brain. All this is littleness—' And with the proofs in her hands that are again in those shameful gloves she makes a gesture. 'Doesn't it chafe you?' cries Miss Dunn.

'Not in the least,' says Selina coldly.

'Treading round. Treading round. No, not even as impressive as treading: *trotting* round and round.'

There is a surprised silence. Selina stares at the dowdy comic old woman. But this can be nothing to do with *me*. Not with me, she cries silently.

'And in the end what is there to show for it,' says Miss Dunn, 'when you are old and perhaps left alone? You haven't been anywhere, done anything, seen anything and there is no time left and you have nothing to remember. You are young Selina but not so young; one day before you notice it, you will be old. I am old. I have often wanted – to speak to you. Oh my dear, why don't you do something before it is too late?'

Lark's eyes, wide with interest, go from one face to the other.

'But – I am always doing things,' cries Selina and her voice sounds suddenly genuine, not as it usually sounds with acquaintances and friends. 'What do you mean?' she says indignantly.

'That is what I mean,' says Miss Dunn sadly. 'You are always busy doing nothing at all. Puffs of empty wind—' says Miss Dunn sadly.

Selina is tempted to laugh, the old woman is so strange and so comic, but she is a little angry. 'I am sorry,' she says stiffly, 'but I shall be late, Miss Dunn. I must go.'

Miss Dunn pays no attention. 'That was why I was always glad to see your dear mother,' she said. 'She knew.'

'*Mother?*'

'Yes. She could never go far from this house but her thoughts were large. She knew this hemmed – this cramped – she at least wanted—' She breaks off under Selina's angry jealous stare, but she is quite certain of what she means. 'I loved your mother,' she says defiantly. 'She was rewarded. She was loved.'

In silence she puts the proofs into her big ridiculous bag with its loops across her arm; she bends her head so that the brim of her dark-grey bonnet – at least twenty years old, thinks Selina angrily – hides her face, but they know she is wiping her eyes. She blows her nose. For a moment longer the bonnet remains bent, then she raises her head. Though her cheeks are patchy and her eyes and her nose are red, her voice is clear as she says, 'I didn't intend – when I came in – but you see Selina, I *know*.'

She goes and the room is still silent and then Lark in her deep interest asks a question. 'Is it so important to be loved?' asks Lark.

Proutie turned away from the dressing-room door. He was bewildered and then across the landing he saw Rolls asleep in the armchair.

'Mr Rolls! Have you been there all night? Oh, Mr Rolls! Sir! That isn't good for you. You haven't been to bed at all. That isn't right.'

Rolls opened his eyes. They were heavy but they had a look of peace, of satisfaction until they saw Proutie standing with the tray.

'Oh, Mr Rolls!'

'What d'you want?' growled Rolls.

'You haven't been to bed, not all night.'

'What the deuce is that to do with you? Go away. I don't want to be disturbed.'

'But it isn't good for you.'

'Good God, my God!' said Rolls. 'Can't I do what I like?'

'Not at your time of life, sir, not without paying for it.'

'It is my life,' Rolls glared. 'At last it is my life, and I shall do in it exactly as I choose, d'you hear?'

'At least have your tea,' said Proutie.

'Blast you Proutie,' said Rolls but he took the tray. 'Very well. Now go away. Go away and keep away, d'you hear?'

Proutie smiled stiffly and went downstairs. Rolls sank back in the chair. He forgot the tea.

There was a ring at the front door.

In the house there are Roly and Rollo as well as Rolls. Selina tries to possess Roly and fails; Rollo is not as easily possessed, though he might have been. Might have been, said Rolls. It was odd how those words recurred. Was Rolls possessed? It was difficult to tell what Rolls had been. Over him there was ruled a long straight honourable – and exceedingly efficient, in spite of its stultified end – straight line; perhaps they were right and it was red tape, a piece of good red tape called a career; pasted down over him, it hid him entirely. There was nothing of that Rolls, the Rolls of those years, to be seen. What was I? What did I do? Where was I? thought Rolls. Where have I been?

He opened his eyes because he thought he had cried out. He was sure he had cried out aloud but there was silence. His eyes were heavy and puffy and old, but the cry he had felt go through him was young and it was far more fresh and cruel than when he had felt it for the first time. But I didn't feel it, said Rolls. I was a young puppy. I couldn't feel. I hadn't the feelings . . . And he could not believe he had not cried out aloud. Lark. Where are you? Where are you Lark? And he asked again, bewildered, Where have I been?

'It was funny,' said her voice in his ear. 'You turned out the most important in the end.'

'Funny!' said Rolls offended. 'What do you mean, funny?'

'I always looked on Pelham as the promising one.'

'Nonsense, my dear Lark.' Rolls was testy. 'Pelham was mostly wind.'

'You were pretty bombastic yourself. I trembled when I heard you had left San Diego and were back at the War Office.'

Rolls had left the War Office in nineteen twenty-five, to become governor of the island of San Diego. He was recalled on the outbreak of war and was firmly retired eleven months later. 'The Great Dane fossil' they called him. He did not care to be reminded of that.

'Thank you. Thank you,' he said. 'And what about you? You belonged to a pretty tattling scandalous set if you like!'

'I know I did.' It was as soft as a sigh, as a reproach, and Rolls stirred in his chair. Then she gently mocked him. 'But if you had forgotten me, and you said you had forgotten me, how did you know?'

There she had him. How did he know? That was his secret, locked away in a drawer in his desk wherever he had been. 'Pshaw!' said Rolls, his moustache and eyebrows moving. 'I used to read about you, Press cuttings; I – collected them of you.'

'And I of you. Oh Rollo! What unhappy wasted lives we both have lived.'

Rolls was slightly nettled. 'Well I don't know that you could describe mine as wasted,' he said, and he added honestly, 'It wasn't unhappy.'

'Nor was mine,' said the Marchesa. 'Now I come to think of it. It sounds unhappy that is all. I enjoyed it very much.'

'So did I. Then – you disappeared.'

'You – noticed?'

These conversations often came like this: sometimes not clear, then every inflection crystal-clear as it was now. 'You – noticed?' He could hear, crystal-clear, the pleasure, the joy in Lark's voice.

'Of course I did,' he said gruffly. 'It made me wonder about you more.'

'I don't believe you.' She was delighted. 'You were too busy. You didn't have time.'

'I have always been absurdly sentimental,' said Rolls.

'Is it sentimental to stay in love?'

'Mr Rolls.'

'Say that again, Lark. Don't go away.'

'*Mr Rolls!*'

'Lark! Lark!'

'Mr Rolls. Sir. I am sorry.'

'Blast you to hell Proutie,' said Rolls opening his eyes.

'I had to disturb you,' said Proutie. '*Miss Dane* has come.'

Rolls looked at Proutie under two horns of eyebrow. 'What?' And then he asked, 'Did you say that, or did I?'

'I did sir. You have been dreaming,' said Proutie. 'I am not speaking of Miss Selina. There is another Miss Dane. You have forgotten. She is Mr Pelham's grand-daughter, Mr Rolls.'

'That was a boy,' objected Rolls. 'My nephew. He is in America.' And he said in alarm, 'We don't want any nephews here.'

'Mr Pelham had a son,' said Proutie patiently, 'but this is further on sir. This is that son's daughter, Mr Rolls.'

'And I thought we were ended: scattered – comfortably finished.'

'I am glad to think not.' Proutie was all smiles.

'Why has she come here? What does she want?'

'She wants to see you. She is in uniform. Some U. S. corps. She must have come over with that.'

'I don't like belligerent women,' said Rolls.

'Now sir,' said Proutie.

'Pantomime,' said Rolls. 'They will have a woman commander-in-chief next, General Boadicea. Pshaw! I hope I am dead.'

'They do splendid work these girls,' said Proutie disapprovingly. If he was exceedingly angry with Rolls Proutie called him 'Sir Roland'. It was on his tongue now.

'And they throw me out! Retire me. "Retire" is a polite word Proutie but it means "thrown out", "disgraced".'

'Disgraced my foot!' said Proutie. 'You wait and see. You see what an obituary notice you will get.'

'I shall not get an obituary notice.'

'You will,' said Proutie unsympathetically. 'Shall I bring her up, Mr Rolls?'

'No.'

'Yes sir.'

'Retired! Candidate for an obituary notice, while this chit of a girl—'

'Goes in to take your place,' said Proutie. 'That is nice sir.'

'Nice! —!'

'That is how it is in families.'

'I wouldn't know,' said Rolls disagreeably. 'I am not a family man.'

'Not lately?' asks Proutie and he says, 'I think she has come to stay. She has brought her luggage.'

'—!*What?*' For a moment words left Rolls.

Then he shouted. 'Tell her to go away. Tell her I shan't see her. Tell her to go, I say.'

'She is a relation,' said Proutie.

'We don't want new relations here. No one, no one, on any pretext is going to force themselves into the house just now.'

'What am I to tell her?' said Proutie.

'What am I telling you? Tell her what is true. That the house is ended. Tell her we are giving up the house. Tell her that it is full. Tell her there is no room.'

Grizel sat in the hall and waited. Occasionally she took out of her pocket a little case that held a mirror and a comb and looked at herself, as if to reassure herself that she was there, the same Grizel. She did not normally need reassurance. She was an independent little cat that walked by itself, very pleasant, very efficient and self-contained. She was successful too; from her training school she had been sent straight on an officer's course and now on her cuffs she wore two stripes. Grizel's universe was usually bright and promising but last night, her first night in London, she had been rattled. *Rattled* is a good word, thought Grizel, looking at the tips of her polished brown shoes. *Rattled.* Everything in the whole of you, in your compos, is shaken and knocked out of place. You don't know where you are. That was a new feeling for Grizel, who always knew exactly where she was.

She had thought she knew what England and London would

be like; and she did not. She had thought that in the night there would be an air raid; and there was not. She had thought she would experience a thrill, and perhaps a little exaltation in that she and her corps, the Americans, had come with their ambulances to help; and she had not. She was thoroughly disconcerted. In her room, in the house in which she was billeted, was a case of stuffed owls; all night when she lay awake wondering for the first time how she, Lieutenant Dane of the U. S. ambulance corps, might, or might not, behave in a raid – and I am only human, thought Grizel – all night the owls watched her with eyes that she knew were only glass and that looked sagely human. She had a feeling, in her confusion, that the owls' eyes were far more human than her own. All night, in her tired confused brain, they asked a question. *Is it you? Is it you? Are you human Grizel Dane?*

Grizel was no more used to being uncomfortable than she was used to being unhappy. If I am not happy, was one of her maxims, I look about for the cause and remove it, or remove myself from the cause. But this time she could not do that. She had decided in the morning that the cause of her feeling uncomfortable was not herself but the owls and, as she could not explain this to her superior officer as a plea for an exchange of billets, she decided to call on her Great-uncle Rolls in Wiltshire Place and ask him to give her a room. I shall be comfortable here, said Grizel, looking round. It seems a nice house. She had no doubt that she could be anything else but acceptable in it.

But she was still not feeling quite happy, in fact she was still feeling unhappy, and she had an increasing feeling that the owls were the symptoms and not the cause. In spite of her maxim she could not find the cause.

Though she liked its colours and shape, the hall looked gloomy to Grizel; it looked grimed, used. But stairs, landings, halls, are more used than any other part of a house, thought Grizel. How did she know? In New York they lived in an apartment on the fifth floor; they never walked upstairs, they used the elevator. Stairs are like roads after all, thought Grizel, and she was surprised at herself. Like roads. A highway, she continued, watching the serpentine twist of the rail out of her sight – *Highways link the tracts of country that are unknown, making them accessible and plain.* She had read that; somewhere; now it came into her head. She looked up the stairway to where the well showed daylight up above. It is all unknown to me, thought Grizel. It is better I start with the stairs.

I can remember my grandfather, she said, but she had difficulty in remembering him because she had never been interested in him; now, by thinking hard, she was able to recall a hand shaking on a cane and a white silk handkerchief and a watch. That old grandfather came down these stairs; perhaps even once upon a time slid down these banisters, and she seemed to see another hand, a boy's that she had not imagined before – never had cause to imagine, said Grizel – a boy's hand, long ago, out of the past. My grandfather. A boy. He came from this house in a direct line. In direct line I have come back.

It seemed to her all at once that the house was immensely bigger than she first had thought; it had, she glimpsed, a common life far greater than the individual little lives that were her grandfather and herself. It held them both. He was dead, she was alive, but there was no difference between them in the house. Grizel did not like that. She was insistent. No. No, she cried. He is dead. It is I, Grizel, who am alive. Then her cheeks warmed. It was as if someone had coldly remarked, 'What a clamour you make Grizel.'

She waited. Down the well of the stairs came voices, and argument. Her great-uncle, it seemed, was not in a hurry to see her. She waited. She listened to the clocks, the vibrating that shook the house when a train went under it; she looked at the hall and at the stair carpet. I wonder how many stair carpets wore out? thought Grizel, but she thought that the brass stair-rods must be the same. She looked at the rods with respect and thought how strange it was that small unnoticeable things should often hold such venerableness. The brass rods went up, one after the other, until they disappeared from sight. They shone. I wonder who keeps them clean?

She had a sudden idea of the labour of this house: the labour against the use, the grime. And not only the actual labour, thought Grizel, but to plan it all so that it and all its lives ran smoothly. She was visited again by the sight of the house as she had first seen it from the outside, as she stepped out of the taxi. It had not seemed large then; just now it seemed big: now it seemed vast – then it suddenly seemed to narrow and become small. Vast at one moment, a cumbersome monster that ate lives; and then small and shut in as if it had barred windows. Grizel gave a shudder. Thank goodness, thank goodness, said Grizel, that I am free.

She stood up and walked calmly and resolutely up the stairs from whence the voices came.

'You can tell her there is no room,' Rolls was saying. 'I-will-not-see-her-do-you-hear?'

'Good morning, Uncle Rollo,' said Grizel.

Rolls stood up slowly and she could see him against the light, a huge old man with thick white hair, thick massive white eyebrows, crumpled collar and a tweed coat. He held the back of the chair he had been sitting in, while he straightened his stiff back, and glowered at her.

Why does he look so cross? thought Grizel. Maybe he has gout.

Ancestors she knew had gout and Rolls was her ancestor, or did ancestors have to be dead? Nowadays you called them people rather than ancestors. That ancestors were people had not dawned on Grizel. She thought he might have gout and she smiled gently and suitably as she said, 'I am very pleased to see you, Uncle Rollo.'

Rolls waited until Proutie had gone before he answered. 'In England we usually wait until we are asked before we walk into people's private rooms.'

'In America too,' Grizel agreed. 'But this isn't a room and I didn't know I should walk straight into it.'

'What is your name?' he asked.

'Grizel.'

'Grizel. Short for Griselda? That is my mother's name.'

'I am not Griselda. I am Grizel.'

'Same thing. Why did they call you that? After her of course. Daft! She is herself, not you.'

'And I,' said Grizel pleasantly, 'am myself too.'

There was a silence. When Grizel considered it had gone on long enough she broke it. 'Uncle Rollo,' she said pleasantly still but firmly, 'you must forgive me for coming so early but I have to report at nine. We only arrived last night.'

'Dear me!' said Rolls. 'You must have been in a great hurry to see me.' Her eyes wavered and she stopped. 'It isn't quite that—'

'I know it isn't,' said Rolls. 'You want something, don't you? I had a letter from your father, now I remember it. I had forgotten. I have so much to think of. Your father said he need not ask me to look after you because you could do that for yourself.'

'I can.'

'He said you would come and see me, if there was anything you wanted. What do you want?' he asked dryly.

Grizel only looked relieved. 'I am not very interested in families and relations,' she said with honesty, looking Rolls straight in the eyes. 'I don't like history or all this bother about the past. I would have come to see you, Uncle Rollo, honest I would. One day I would have come, but I have come now because I want you to give me a room and let me stay here. My billet is impossible, Uncle Rollo. I shall go crazy if I stay there one more night.'

'If you are in the Army,' said Rolls disagreeably, 'and I suppose you consider yourself in the Army, you take what billets you are given. You don't go turning up your nose at this and that. You have to make the best of what you are given in the Army.'

'Yes. When it is necessary,' said Grizel in her same unmoved soft polite voice. 'How many rooms have you in the house?'

Rolls's eyebrows twitched.

'Your man, Proutie, that is his name, isn't it, told me there were only the two of you in the house. Only you and he.'

'Did he?' said Rolls. 'Nevertheless all the rooms in this house belong to somebody else.'

'But they are *empty*! Why shouldn't I come? It is the family house. I belong to the family.'

'And you have only just thought of that haven't you?' said Rolls. 'You have never thought of it before. You didn't think of it when you came. All you wanted was to get out of an uncomfortable place and make yourself comfortable. You didn't for one moment think of the house.'

'But – does one think of houses?' asked Grizel.

'I know you.' Rolls was angry. 'I know you. You will go all over it and poke into every corner and discover and piece together and ask questions and want answers. I know you.'

'I shall when I have time,' answered Grizel, surprised. 'Why shouldn't I? Isn't it natural? Is there any reason why I shouldn't? Has anything happened here, Uncle Rolls? Anything unusual?'

'To be born and to live and to die is quite usual,' said Rolls. And he added, 'We have to leave the house in any case.'

'When?' said Grizel with curious consternation.

'When? Shortly.' Rolls dodged the question. 'It wouldn't be worth your coming.'

'Let me come,' said Grizel.

'We don't want to be disturbed. Do you know what you would be?' he flung at her – 'A discord.'

'I shouldn't be,' said Grizel steadily. 'I should complete the chord.'

Rolls was silent for a moment; then: 'Come here into the light,' he said, 'and let me see how you look.'

Grizel came up to him. He seemed hugely tall as she stood beside him. He was above her in front of the window. The light fell on her face.

'You have Pelham's narrow head,' said Rolls, 'and you have his hair, that mouse-brown stuff. Selina had it too, and all the others. Mine was chestnut. That is a real colour. Your chin is your own, and your mouth.' He put his hand under her chin and turned her face up, and his touch was not like an old man's, an uncle's, a great-uncle's; it was warm and vivifying. It surprised Grizel. What a blood he must have been, thought Grizel and clearly, like a bell ringing in her mind, she was corrected: *Not a blood. Not a blood, but a blade.* What a blade he must have been – and aloud she said softly 'Uncle Rollo!' and blushed.

'Rollo was my name when I was young,' said Rolls. 'I had forgotten it – till lately. It is a pretty mouth Grizel. Keep it pretty. Don't be too hard on it. Don't be a shrew. I think you are a little shrew you know. Don't be too efficient – or self-sufficient. You are a woman.' And he added, 'You have Griselda's eyes. I never saw them but they are in the painting of her downstairs.'

'You have them too,' said Grizel.

She was remembering something. It was the picture of Rolls in the illustrated paper with the six German generals opposite. In the American edition it was coloured and she remembered how blue his eyes had been; if their gaze was not as straight as Griselda's, it was straight enough.

'*Who is the old buster?*'

'*My great-uncle, General Dane.*'

'*He looks as if he had swallowed a harpoon.*'

'*He doesn't look as if he had swallowed a harpoon!*' She had said that with furious indignation, that surprised herself as much as it surprised them, because that was the first time she had ever paid any attention to the fact of her Great-uncle Rollo. At that moment, a crack opened in her feelings that had up to then been so perfectly firm and consolidated and cemented that nothing Grizel did not plan could enter into them. She had managed to control herself and say judiciously, '*I prefer him to these,*' and she had looked at the Germans. '*Their heads are full of bumps; yes, they look bumptious. I like the shape of my old General's head.'*

It was exactly the same shape as her own. A month later she volunteered for the ambulance corps.

Now Rolls was turning her face up to the light, studying it. 'You make me sound like a patchwork,' said Grizel.

'Not patchwork. Hotchpotch,' said Rolls gravely. 'A hotch-potch of us all. Of all that have been in this house.'

'Then how could I be a discord? Uncle Rollo, let me come.'

He moved away from her and went to the bookcase near the wall and rang the bell. 'It will be your own fault if you do,' he said. 'Don't complain about it afterwards.'

'Why should I complain?'

'There is very little room,' said Rolls. 'You will have to fit into your place. You can't be so' – he looked at her – 'self-contained. You won't be alone, you will find. You may even lose yourself and you won't like that.'

'I don't understand,' said Grizel.

'All you young people think you are so complete,' said Rolls.

Complete? What a funny word to use, thought Grizel.

'Nothing is complete. You are only limited. Nothing is certain. We have to leave this house. It is all only a lease of occupation,' said Rolls. 'It – you – are only another phase. You must remember that.'

'Do you?' asked Grizel.

'N-no,' Rolls answered slowly, and then he said defiantly, 'I am an old man. I know what I am doing.' He looked at Grizel challengingly.

What is he trying to do? she wondered. What is happening to him? She was not experienced in her dealings with the elderly. She had always eschewed them, avoided them carefully; they were crotchety she understood, required to be humoured, had to have excuses made for them, be helped and waited on; all these things she had no wish to do and she had avoided them. Now Uncle Rolls, Great-uncle Rolls, stood up and challenged her and he had a touch that made her, Grizel, the cool contained experienced Grizel, capable of handling a hundred bushmen – or, more dangerous, one bushman – she, Grizel, had blushed.

'Listen,' said Rolls, 'because I shall not explain this again. There are these people in, connected with, the house: first there is my father, your great-grandfather, John Ironmonger Dane. Ironmonger is a family name, not an occupation. We called him "the Eye".'

'Why?'

'My mother called him that, "*Thou God seest me.*" She married him when she was seventeen. I have never been able to make up my mind,' said Rolls, 'if she were unhappy or not. I don't think she could make that out either. Perhaps she knew how to be both. Pelham, your grandfather, was their eldest son. I remember thinking when he was my guardian that he could never have been a child, he was so sedate. There isn't a trace of him here as a child or a boy. Funny! There were four more brothers but they are not here either, but they were sent to school very young. Then came Selina, my eldest sister; Lena she was called as a child. Then there were the twins. Griselda had too many children but I believe she set her heart on one, on the second twin Elizabeth. They died of diphtheria when they were five years old. I never knew them. I was born two years later and Griselda died when I was born. That is all, not counting the servants of course, and of course they are very important. That is all that is necessary for you to know.'

'Necessary?' asked Grizel puzzled.

'Yes. The Eye; Griselda; Pelham; Selina; the twins; me. That is all that it is necessary for you to know.'

Proutie had come up and was waiting by Rolls's elbow. Now he said, as if he had not heard Rolls, 'Which room shall I give Miss Grizel, Mr Rolls? Miss Selina's, or would she go upstairs in the night nursery like Miss Lark? Perhaps Miss Selina's would be better,' he added quickly catching the look on Rolls's face.

'Lark?' asked Grizel. 'You didn't tell me about Lark. What a beautiful name – why didn't you tell me about her?'

'Put Miss Grizel in Miss Selina's room,' said Rolls. 'Go and look at it with Proutie please Grizel.'

'But who was Lark?' asked Grizel. 'I want to know.'

Her question was not answered. Proutie led the way towards Selina's room to the far right of the landing. Rolls turned from her to the window. The question hung on the air. Grizel waited. After a moment she followed Proutie towards the door.

NOON

Grizel occupied Selina's room. That exactly expressed it. She could not feel it was her own.

It had not been closed. It was dusted, almost ready; it had taken Proutie only a few minutes to arrange it for Grizel. It was white, it was prim; it was full of a clutter of things but the effect of it was chilly and strangely empty. Even when Proutie had cleared the mantelpiece and dressing-table to make room for Grizel, when she had put her clothes in the cupboard, her shoes on the little shoe-shelf along the wall, her jars and bottles on the dressing-table, her washcloths and toothbrush on the heavy marbled washing stand with the willow-pattern china, when she had put out her photographs and books, and laid down her gas mask and greatcoat on the ottoman, still the room did not belong to Grizel. It was still Selina's room.

I think this Selina must have taken some defying, thought Grizel. The impression of her was still so strong. But perhaps she was more in the house than the others; girls in those days were so much more in the house, closed into it. Selina was probably

71

born here, thought Grizel, and lived here all her life. Most houses change, she thought. Most houses don't keep the same inhabitants for generations, especially not in towns. The life in them changes and ebbs and flows; the rooms change; they are not usually, for as long as this, one person's room. Life does not stay in them as life has stayed in this. She tried to think of the house as it would be when they had all gone, but she could not. We have to go, said Grizel, but the words seemed to have no credibility or truth; she said them, but she could not believe them.

The room opened on the landing, on the narrow end of it above the stairs. The landing led forward and widened into its sitting-room alcove. There Grizel liked to sit and sew and think. She preferred sewing to reading, because it was not easy to read there she found. She could not concentrate; she was interrupted, though no one interrupted her, and she continually lost her place.

Grizel's unit had been posted to Metropolitan London, and for the first fortnight they had been learning it, learning it so that they could drive it at night with no lights, even under bombing. It seemed incredibly difficult to Grizel. Day followed day and she was giddy with it, with the maze of little streets and the big streets that were still narrow, overtopped with houses and the names interwoven with variations of each other: Wiltshire Square and Wiltshire Crescent; Wiltshire Road, Wiltshire Gardens; Wiltshire Place – all close together except Wiltshire Road, which was the other end of London. Now Grizel had begun to drive by night. By day the huge glossy American ambulance that moved with only a gentle slippery swishing noise of tyres loomed large in the streets; by night the streets enclosed it and its silence seemed part of a dream in which Grizel herself was disembodied. 'Do it once or twice and you get used to it,' said the girl who was with her, an English girl lent by a sister corps. 'I came up from the country myself. Soon you are used to it.' Grizel did not think she would be ever used to it.

She returned in the small hours to the silent house, letting herself in by the latch-key Rolls had given her, shutting out the dark and silence outside for the darkness and silence indoors. As she closed the front door, the quietness of the house closed round her and she found herself listening, her head still giddy from that uncertain dark maze of streets that she had threaded by the powerful wheels under her fingers' control; that power seemed to stay in her fingers after the car was put away. She came in always a little above herself, a little more than Grizel, and as she stood on the mat, the quietness closed round her and seemed to put her back in her place, but – in a smaller place than she was accustomed to know as her own. She found herself listening, watching the shadows, treading uncertainly, as she went up to bed, and then even her room was not her own: it had been Selina's and was Selina's still.

In her time off she did not go out. She did not want, she felt, to see any more of those streets and the house drew her like a magnet. She liked to take her sewing to the landing window and sit there on the window sill. Proutie came up and plugged in the electric fire.

'The heating is on, Proutie.'

'You look peaked Miss Grizel and I know your people keep their houses very warm. There is a draught just here. Miss Selina used always to need a shawl. Of course we didn't have electricity then. Mr Rolls had it put in with the heating even though he wasn't here. He always took a great pride in the house, though when he was in London he stayed at his club or at the Little Regency Hotel in the Square. He kept it up wonderfully. It doesn't seem possible Miss Grizel that we really are to go. He says he won't have anything to do with it when I ask him about the arrangements and time is getting on. He just says, "Do what you think. I won't be here." I am arranging to put everything in store till we see what will happen, but it doesn't seem possible miss.'

'Isn't there anything to be done about it?'

'Young Mr Willoughby of our solicitors miss, though he isn't what you would really call young, he must be fifty, he says they are trying their best. They can get a short lease, a lease of occupation but he, Mr Rolls, won't take that.'

'A lease of occupation,' said Grizel thoughtfully, and she asked, 'So Selina sat here?' She was not it seemed to get away from Selina.

'The first Mr Dane, Mr Rolls's father, had it furnished like this for Mrs Dane. He was always doing something for her, changing her room colours or bringing back something from his office for her, my auntie said. She was cook here and used often to describe her. Miss Selina liked to sit at the table with her letters and accounts and that, but Mrs Dane, my auntie told me, would sit here where you are, looking out.

'If you had seen the Place then,' said Proutie, 'it would not have been so quiet. It used to be more fashionable. If you had sat there then, you would have seen carriages stopping at the door, and driving out to the Park in the afternoons, and in the evening standing at the doors with their lamps lit all along the kerb. I have passed them and looked inside and seen the dark green seats and the ivory tabs on the window blinds, and the shine on the panels and the horses' flanks where the light caught them; there is a wonderful smell to a carriage Miss Grizel, not like the stink of a car. And there would be delivery vans, light green and drab and mustard and olive-green and the coachmen in livery to match; yes, some of the shops kept wonderful smart turnouts. There were the milliner girls with their boxes and the hawkers; the strawberry sellers and the shrimp woman in the summer, and in the winter, coals and country logs and chestnuts; and there was the muffin-and-crumpet man,' said Proutie. 'He would come round about tea-time and you would hear his bell. And at night you would hear the watchman: every night you would hear him. He had a noisy old rattle but his calling the hours was comforting to people who couldn't sleep, people who were up late in trouble or pain. *"Twelve o'clock. A starry night. All's well."* I wish we had him now instead of the syren, don't you Miss Grizel?'

'But,' said Grizel, 'but, Proutie, *you* don't remember all that?'

'Don't I?' Proutie looked uncertain. 'No, of course I don't. I don't know what made me reel it off like that. I suppose I am not sure what I remember and what I have been told. My auntie used to bring me over here as a child. The house was a kind of Mecca to me. I was in the convent orphanage over the way and every time I went in or out with the Sisters I used to look across and know I should come here one day. I was boy first, then footman and then when Slater died I stepped straight into his shoes. I loved it from the first day. The house was like a hive then; as I remember it, it used to hum from top to bottom, but I remember thinking that the further up the house you went the quieter it became. The kitchen was full, the family was not large but there were always visitors and guests, but at the top there was only Miss Lark and she made hardly a sound.'

'Proutie, who was Lark? I want to know.'

'She was Mr Dane's ward,' said Proutie slowly.

'John Ironmonger Dane?'

'Yes, miss, Mr Dane. She ran away.'

'Oh Proutie! Why?'

'There were a lot of stories,' said Proutie evasively.

'Didn't she ever come back?'

'No,' said Proutie. 'It is funny. No one ever made less stir in a house as far as you could see than she did but nothing was ever more felt than when she went. She was happy in herself I think,' said Proutie. 'She used to sing. I suppose we listened more than we knew. I never knew what happened to her except for the bits we used to read in the illustrated papers, and see her photographs.' He thought for a moment and then said with resentment in his voice, 'I used to ask Miss Selina for news of her. "Is there any news of Miss Lark?" and she always said, "None whatever Proutie. None." Miss Selina didn't like even to speak of her.'

Softly and evenly from St Benedict's, the clock on the steeple struck twelve. A moment after the sound came from another clock further away, and another and another, and after them the grandfather clock in the hall struck, too; then faintly they heard the chimes of the clocks downstairs, dining-room, study; the drawing-room clock was always too gentle to hear outside the room.

'There was one more,' said Proutie. 'On the nursery landing. A cuckoo clock that used to come after them all. It grew later and later and then it broke and somehow it never was mended. Well, it is twelve o'clock already. I must get on. You will be in to lunch Miss Grizel?'

'No, I have to be down at two,' said Grizel. 'I can get lunch in the canteen.'

'I can manage it for you easily,' said Proutie.

'No, I will go, thank you Proutie. I don't know how you do manage,' said Grizel. 'Only you in this great house.'

'There were six servants living in,' said Proutie, 'not counting the nursery and schoolroom staff. But I have Mrs Crabbe. You will get to know that our London charladies are an institution Miss Grizel. Why we used to have her grandmother, old Mrs Sampson.'

'Everything here, even the charwoman, seems to link up with something else,' Grizel complained. 'Nothing seems to be only itself in England.'

'Sometimes when I am working now,' said Proutie suddenly, 'I feel that I am not doing only what I am doing but what has been done before; as if a thousand hands were working there with mine. It is a good feeling Miss Grizel, as if you were not doing only your petty little part but something common – big. I seem to hear that humming again. It is like a hum from a hive. I have almost run upstairs expecting to find – well I couldn't say quite what, but it would be a shock to find the stillness empty.' And he said slowly, 'It is noticeable since Mr Rolls came back. Came back here to live. When he was retired, he turned from everyone and everything and hid himself here. I was worried. You see all these years he was so active and so important Miss Grizel. His work and his responsibility, they occupied all his time and thoughts; they took the whole of him and then they were taken away at one blow. He came back here with nothing to do all day long but brood.'

'Is he brooding?' asked Grizel. 'He doesn't brood.'

'No he doesn't,' said Proutie. 'But why not? I don't know what he is up to. There was only he and I and Mrs Crabbe in the house: no one else came ever. He wouldn't see anyone. No one else, I am sure of that.' He turned to Grizel. 'You don't know how glad I am that you have come miss. We need you. The house needs you.'

'Needs me? But I have promised not to interfere.'

'You won't be able to help it,' said Proutie. 'A house recognizes its own.'

'Oh Proutie!'

'I believe it does,' says Proutie stoutly. 'And now, more than ever, because of you Miss Grizel, I can't believe that it is going to end.'

When Proutie had gone downstairs Grizel continued to sew. She had another three quarters of an hour before she need get ready. She sat looking down into the Place, thinking of it as Proutie had told her and she had a sense of the different parts of the house. She felt as if invisible threads were fastened from different places in it to her; some of the threads vibrated easily, some hung slackly and some jerked actually, yet for Grizel nothing that was happening in any part of the house was her concern; even the lunch that Proutie was cooking in the kitchen was not for her; she had refused it. She was herself, apart; nothing that happened in the study or drawing-room or dining-room or front door or hall or bedrooms or nursery or kitchens was any concern of hers; yet, as she sat in the window-seat, she was caught firmly in the web of it.

Isn't this what I might feel, asked Grizel, if I had a husband in the study, children in the nursery, servants in the kitchen, visitors and letters and notes and parcels at the front door? If I were Griselda? Heaven help me, thought Grizel, I don't want to be Griselda. I want to be myself, free, not entangled with all this, with anyone.

She had a sudden idea that, if she sat there, she might be Selina. She laid down her sewing and went to the chair and sat down and, though perhaps it was her imagination, she had immediately the thought that she must speak to the cook about the leg of pork.

Not leg – loin, came the bell in her mind.

Loin, said Grizel going back to the window-seat. I wonder how many notes Griselda had to write in a year. Why should she, Grizel wondered, wonder that? Notes: a note for So-and-so to come and dine, a note of acceptance to dine with So-and-so, a thank-you note for a present of game, an invitation to be accepted for a children's party, a refusal for another; and memorandum notes written in a notebook: to return a call, to buy this, to buy that, to take something home on approval, to return something else; it must have taken time, thought Grizel, time and thinking to deal with all those notes. She was suddenly and vividly sorry for Griselda. She thought of her going to an endless formal dinner party in a grey moire dress, an enormous crinoline, with an under-ruche of lace and crimson velvet roses.

Not crimson roses – moss, corrected the bell.

Moss? Did Griselda suit moss roses? Perhaps she did. Moss roses are overlaid with close green, green because it is perpetually renewed, countless tiny hairs of moss that bind the rose: duty, love and friendship, order and achievement, food and drink, linen and clothes and medicine, discipline, manners and lessons, charities, going to church, musical evenings, and calling and dinners and dancing and visiting and driving and shopping, listening, agreeing and listening again. Grizel had included almost everything for Griselda except thinking. 'Gentle,' murmured Grizel aloud. 'Gentle, soft-spoken, soft-tempered and dutiful—'

Beautiful – not dutiful, came the bell.

Grizel was surprised. That did not seem in order with her notions of a Victorian wife. Grizel had, as for most things, a pigeonhole in her mind for a Victorian wife, but it seemed, in spite of the firmness of her thoughts, that her great-grandmother Griselda would not quite fit into it. Beautiful – not dutiful. It sounded rebellious. A doubt disturbed Grizel. Did Griselda rebel? Did she feel, of all this, much as I feel? Did she want to be nonattached as I do? As I am? Then why, why did she submit?

It could not have been easy in her day to rebel. Probably she had a father who – probably she didn't have a real will of her own. But didn't she? As if Griselda had smiled, Grizel felt her suppositions to be impertinent and a little crude. Griselda had submitted. Perhaps she chose to. Perhaps she gave herself to the Eye and her children and to the house. 'Well I wouldn't,' said Grizel aloud. 'I can see no sense in it. I won't give myself away to anyone.' But this morning she had experienced a little of what it was like to be Griselda; to be Selina. She was not, this morning, only herself, Grizel.

Into the quietness of the house as she sewed came the sound of a cuckoo clock; it struck twelve times – cuckoo cuckoo cuckoo cuckoo cuckoo cuckoo cuckoo cuckoo cuckoo cuckoo cuckoo cuckoo – and sank with a whirr to be quiet again.

It is a bitter dull morning thick with fog at twelve o'clock on a January day. The fog has not lifted for two days, thick and yellow, and the gas lamps have burned in the streets all the time. This morning it is worse than ever. The air is raw and in the house the windows are tightly sealed and fires are lit. Though it is only twelve o'clock Pelham has come in after trying since ten to reach the City. Jamieson the coachman has just been told to put the horses away and Proutie has gone in front of them to light them with a torch.

Pelham comes into the drawing-room where Selina has rung the bell for sherry and plum-cake. Slater brings it on a silver tray: a plate of cake, dark and heavy and rich, its spiced smell filling the fire-warmed air; three glasses and decanter full of clear gold-brown wine from the last six dozen of Amontillado the Eye laid down before he died.

'I shall go upstairs,' says Selina. 'I shall just go upstairs and put on a jacket. It *is* cold this morning isn't it? Agnes is busy with my dress for to-night though it doesn't look as if we should be able to go. That reminds me—'

She goes out and Pelham hears her high clear tones asking Slater in the hall, 'Hasn't Miss Lark come in yet?' and he hears the annoyance in her voice as she says, 'This isn't giving Agnes a chance.'

Lark? Is the child out in this? thinks Pelham, but concern does not really touch him. Lark is only a wraith to Pelham, an irritating wraith who has to be paid for. He stands with the fire warming his legs, and looks out of the warm gracious room to the garden outside; he can see the red chairs, the moving fire reflected in the glass, but the fog shuts off the garden in a thick green saffron mist. The child shouldn't be out, thinks Pelham mildly and he stretches his feet in his warm slippers comfortably. There is something novel and carefree in being at home in the middle of the morning when it is not Sunday or a holiday. There is something extra cosy in being in this room full of warmth and colour and a fragrance that is made up of the smell of apple wood from the burning logs, and of violets from the winter bowl on the writing desk, and of polish from the furniture and parquet, and of wine and rich plum-cake. Pelham does not often expand but now he feels large and genial. He sips his sherry and stands by the fire with its warmth on his legs that are covered neatly with speckled grey trousers; he is a neat small man with neat brown hair brushed back from his forehead; he is sedate and inclined to be pompous, very timid and careful over money, but he is kind.

The door opens suddenly and it is Lark. Before she looks into the room she says in the breathless tired voice, 'Selina I couldn't get the silk. I couldn't.' She sees Pelham and breaks off at once.

Pelham, with his wine-glass in his hand, stares at her.

She is soaked. She has been lost in the fog for two hours and she is white with cold and her eyes are large with fright. Her eyes seem enormous to Pelham – like anemones, those flowers with black centres, he thinks suddenly and suddenly also he thinks that she looks like a nymph, a water nymph with her wetness and her whiteness and her hair clinging round her forehead. He sees how tall she is, how fully curved in the clinging sodden coat. What curves, thinks Pelham, and what a mouth! It is trembling now but what a full red bow! A nymph? thinks Pelham. Why the child is a perfect goddess! 'Lark!' he says aloud. 'Why Lark! I thought you were still a little girl.'

'Isn't S-Selina here?' asks Lark and he sees that she is shivering.

'Come here. Come to the fire at once,' he says.

'I c-can't. I'm s-soaking.'

'Come along at once. Take off your coat.'

'Can I? I am c-cold.'

'Come. Come.' He puts down his glass as she comes. She is taller than he as she stands beside him. She holds out her hands and he sees that they are small for her height and finely shaped though they are red with cold; he also sees that her coat-sleeves are so short that they are halfway up her wrist. 'Take off that coat!' he says. 'My dear child, you are wringing wet. Where have you been?'

'S-Selina sent me out for some silk she wanted for Agnes to finish her dress, but I c-couldn't find my way even as far as Oxford Street.'

Pelham does not answer. She has taken off her coat and her dark blue cap and he sees that her hair is still down, hanging to her waist, and that its darkness looks darker still because of the sparks of wetness in it; that wetness clings to her lashes too, dividing them into points. That is why her eyes look so big, thinks Pelham. Well there are black fringes in anemones. He looks at her and the words shape themselves in his head: Nymph. Nymph. Dearest nymph.

'Do you mind if I kneel down?' asks Lark politely. 'It is warmer.'

She kneels down and Pelham is more at ease, less taken aback, as soon as he can look down on her head.

'I am going to give you a glass of wine,' he says.

'O-oh!' Lark's eyes light up. 'But won't Selina mind?'

'It doesn't matter if she does,' says Pelham jauntily and he pours out a glass of sherry and cuts a heavy slice of cake for her. Then he sits down feeling the fire on his face.

Lark is wearing a dress that, though he sees it is old, has colours that are beautiful for her; it is a faded rubbed dress of amethyst-coloured velvet that gives her eyes a darker violet blue; it has a fitting bodice, a little too fitting because it is growing too tight and Pelham finds his eyes keep straying to Lark's breasts, rounded and breathing as she leans forward to warm her hands. Her skirt is turned back to show an underskirt, a fisher-girl skirt in stripes of purple and black. She has black stockings and black shoes and, in the sole of one shoe shown as she kneels, there is a large crack; Pelham looks at it and he feels guilty but at the same time he notices that it is a small shoe; small hands and feet, he says as he looks again at the beautiful curve of her breast rising to her throat. 'Are your feet wet?' he asks sharply with concern. 'You mustn't get a cold. You have a hole in your shoe.'

She looks back over her shoulder at it, turning her neck. 'Oh well, they are old shoes,' she says reasonably, and Pelham feels a deep twinge of shame.

'Does Selina often send you out on errands?' he demands.

'Of course,' says Lark but she adds in extreme fairness, 'but quite often she sends Agnes.'

'You – and Agnes!' Pelham cannot remember feeling as unpleasantly and pleasantly stirred. 'When did you grow up like this Lark?'

'I have been growing up steadily all the time,' answers Lark, wiping the tips of her fingers on her skirt. She is losing her whiteness and the heat of the fire is giving a flush to her face like rose on ivory. 'Do you think I could have some more cake Pelham? It is such heavenly cake.'

Pelham, as he hands it to her, feels gloomy; his gloom is compounded of feeling old and of jealousy and of a sense of hopelessness and this sense of shame; and with these is a weakness that he cannot help, as if he were sliding down some place that was too steep for him, and with it all a strange excitement. 'How old are you?' he asks.

'I am seventeen,' says Lark, and she looks at him under her eyelashes, a look that is as mature as it was childish when she asked him for more cake. 'Seventeen is grown-up,' she says, and as she looks at him Pelham's blood seems to run more quickly and boisterously.

The door opens again and Selina comes in. Her face hardens and her eyebrows go up when she sees Lark kneeling by the fire. Lark makes a movement to stand up but Pelham puts his hand on her shoulder and presses her down. Her shoulder is warm and firm and smooth under his hand.

'I c-couldn't get your silk,' says Lark.

'Couldn't? Why not?'

'I couldn't find the way. You don't know what it was like Selina. I could barely move a step and a man spoke to me, followed me. I was frightened.'

'Frightened! A great girl like you!'

'Well a policeman came and took me part of the way and told me to go home,' says Lark. 'Truly, it was frightening.'

'And I suppose it doesn't matter if my dress isn't finished for to-night.'

Lark is silent. Her lashes are on her cheek as she looks at the fire. Pelham is silent too, watching, waiting for them to lift.

'And may *I* not have a glass of sherry?' asks Selina. 'Lark you have taken my glass.'

'There were three glasses.'

'Rollo said he might drop in if he could find his way through this.'

'Rollo?' Pelham sees the quick upward flicker of Lark's eyes, the flash of blue, and again he has that unaccountable pang.

'Rollo?' he says sourly. 'What is he doing in town?'

'He said he had to fit a pair of boots.'

'Can't he get boots in Worcestershire?'

'Fetch another glass.' Selina's voice when she speaks to Lark is accustomed to be peremptory. She does not realize herself how harsh it sounds. Lark, when she is near her, seems to become younger, to shrink and become utterly docile, without a trace of the maturity she showed to Pelham. She seems to be in hiding. 'And take your things,' says Selina. 'You needn't come back here.'

Lark does not go. She stands up slowly on the hearthrug by Pelham and faces Selina and she does not go. Selina pours out another glass of sherry and then she glances up. Pelham thinks she does not glance up until she is ready. Then she asks, 'What do you want?'

'I don't see,' says Lark, 'why one person should have food like this and another in the same house have food like mine.'

'And what is wrong with your food?'

'It is too young for me.'

It is a surprising answer and she goes on: 'I am not really talking about food Selina and neither are you. I am seventeen. I am too old to be shut away any more. Shut out. I should come out of the schoolroom now. Pelham thinks I should come out.'

'*Pelham?*'

'Yes. Pelham,' Lark answers calmly. And again she gives Pelham that look, mature and intimate from under her lashes and again it gives Pelham a titivation of the blood in all his veins and in his heart. Selina sees it too, and bright quick redness, a sign of anger with Selina, comes into her neck and cheeks.

'Yes,' says Pelham. 'Yes, I think she should come out.'

'Why?' Selina's voice is cutting.

'She is hardly a schoolgirl any longer Lena dear.'

'No?' asks Selina. 'She looks like one.' Her eyes travel slowly and scornfully over Lark. 'An inky finger; muddy shoes; that poor old dress. Really Lark, what do you *do* with your clothes?'

'I never have new ones, decent ones.'

'And a hole in your stocking. No,' says Selina, 'I am afraid I can't agree. Lark is hardly ready for the drawing-room. There is another thing,' says Selina. 'A thing you might have thought of for yourself. I am sure I should have in your place but you were always insensitive. That isn't your fault of course. It is your breeding.'

'My breeding?' Lark does not quite understand, then she asks, 'What is wrong with my breeding?'

'Well,' says Selina with a little laugh. 'It is rather delicate to put into words.'

'You have never been delicate. Please say what you have to, Selina.'

'Your parents were provincial singers. We can hardly expect fineness, too much niceness from you. You are their daughter in spite of your advantages of upbringing.'

'My advantages of upbringing!' Pelham, watching, sees Lark's eyes burn with temper and he sees her hands clench the folds of her dress.

'As I say, were you more sensitively bred, your one desire, when you do leave the schoolroom, would be to try and repay something of what you have received, not to make claims for more.'

'Selina, really I am not going to – Really I must—'

'One minute Pelham. Hush please.' Lark holds up her hand. 'I must say something first, something about these advantages of upbringing.' Her voice is very clear in the room that is quieter than usual from the silence of the fog. 'Of my upbringing and my education, only there wasn't any education. The Eye gave you, Selina, responsibility for that. I can remember my mother,' says Lark. 'She was a singer. She sang, as you say, Selina, in the provinces, in little towns, sometimes twice in a night. It was a provincial town she was travelling to, the night that she was killed – from Stirling to Dundee. I often look at them on the map. She was a provincial singer, but the Eye gave me her albums and her books; he had some of them and her press notices were in them. If she hadn't married my father she might have been a great singer. She sang in Milan and Rome and Paris and London. I can remember her,' says Lark. 'She went to school. She spoke four languages, and sang in them; she played three instruments; she painted. Though she had none of your advantages of upbringing, Selina, she did all these things and she was beautiful and witty. And what can I do? I have taught myself a little from your old books, but I have not had a paid lesson, a lesson that had to be paid for, since I came here. You are always telling me, Selina, how lucky I am to be here. Perhaps the Eye meant it to be lucky, but you haven't made it so. Why,

Harry Proutie is better-educated than I am. You tell me I must repay you. How can I repay you? You wouldn't even give me singing lessons. There is nothing at all that I can do.'

'You are quite useful in the house,' says Selina quite unmoved. 'You can sew. Agnes taught you that quite nicely. You can answer notes. You can be trusted, sometimes, to do shopping. You could be a companion, or, not a governess of course, but a children's maid.'

'A children's maid!' It comes back a whisper into the room.

'Yes,' says Selina. She watches Lark's face with a curious satisfaction. 'You have a great opinion of yourself, haven't you Lark?'

Lark stands a moment longer. Any defence from her is new; she has not learned that she too has power; at the moment Selina's is overwhelming. Lark also is never to be good at fighting; she does not fight, her battles are fought for her. Pelham will fight one for her in a minute and he will win and Selina will not forget nor forgive Lark for that. Lark is right; she does nothing, there is nothing at all that she can do, but as she grows she develops a genius for being.

Long ago one spring afternoon she is sent out with her tea, a slice of bread and jam, to be out of the way in the garden. The house is being spring-cleaned and Proutie, on holiday from the convent orphanage, has to help to clean the windows. He climbs down his ladder from the study windows and stands beside Lark.

'I hate the spring,' says Proutie, who is then called Harry. 'I hate the spring,' says Harry. 'Nothin' but cleanin'.'

Lark knows almost as little about the spring as he does but she knows that this is wrong. 'Oh no Harry,' she says. 'No.' She looks doubtfully at his boots as if she thinks his understanding may be as thick, and she searches for some unfailingly simple way of conveying to him what she feels he ought to know about the spring. She looks first at her own bread and jam. 'Spring is being able to come out of doors after the winter, not to have to walk about but to dawdle and stand still and eat your tea.' She looks up at the window he has just cleaned and at the sparrows in the gutter. 'It is seeing the sun on the windows again and feeling it getting warmer, and it is the birds not coming for crumbs because they can feed themselves and are too busy making their nests. It is in those buds,' she says, waving her bread and jam towards the plane-tree, and she looks down at the garden beds and sees that the lilies of the valley have shoots of pale-green leaves. 'It is in them,' she says. 'Presently they will open into bells, they are a bit smutty but they have a lovely smell.'

'What are they?' asks Harry.

'Lilies,' says Lark.

'Lilies?' asks Harry in surprise. 'So small! I always thought lilies was enormous.' And convent-taught, he surprises Lark who is taught nothing at all. '*Consider the lilies . . .,*' says Harry Proutie; '*they toil not neither do they spin . . . yet . . . Solomon in all his glory was not arrayed like one of these.*'

Lark is surprised and humbled. She remembers what she thought or took for granted from the thickness of his boots. She considers the lilies. She also from that day considers other people rather more. The lilies are perhaps the beginning of her career; her manner of life. 'Solomon's lilies', she always calls them afterwards. One of the things that most annoy Selina is that Lark grows up so like them.

But now Selina's taunts have pierced to her. In spite of herself tears come into her eyes. In a moment she is blind and she puts out her hand, tries to say something more, and chokes and runs out of the room.

After she has gone there is silence except for the noise of the fire and, from somewhere outside, the noise of a bell ringing in the fog. The clock sounds on the mantelpiece and Pelham bends forward and picks up the poker and stirs the fire. 'You are unkind,' says Pelham.

Selina gives a shrug.

'And you are wrong. She is deeply sensitive, deeply.'

'How do you know?'

'I can see. She is a young girl, just unfolding—'

'How poetical you are Pelham dear.'

Pelham is not a poet but he knows what a poet feels like; he has often a poetical nostalgia that he inherits, as well as from Griselda, from the Eye; it is in the Eye's yearning after Griselda and the mother of Lark, after rubies and warm colours; it is in Griselda's vision, in her love of foreign words and things; Rollo has it as well. Pelham has never given rein to it, he is too timid and conventional to give full rein to anything, but it stirs him at moments still. Now he slowly reddens. 'You have a horrid tongue, Selina.' And then an incongruous little memory comes to him. 'Lena,' he asks, 'do you remember your mouse?'

'My mouse? What mouse?'

'A dead mouse you found on the stairs and tried to keep. You kept it in your pocket for days and then Nurse made you throw it away. You cried and clung to it and wouldn't give it up and she forced it out of your hand. Don't you remember it Lena?'

'No I don't,' says Selina. 'Why did I want to keep it if it were dead?'

'You have forgotten,' says Pelham. 'Never mind. It doesn't matter. Selina, I have to speak to you about Lark . . . '

The mention of Lena's mouse, that exists though she has forgotten it, brings out all the mice in the house; real mice: the mice that fiddle on the nursery curtains; a china mouse that ornaments the handle of the servants' cheese dish; a clockwork mouse with its wheels gone wrong that is thrown away in the dustbin; an adventurous mouse that drowns itself in the cistern and costs the Eye forty-two shillings before it is found and removed. The house is full of mice. They have mouse passages behind the wainscot, they abide in the attics, and abound in the cellars; at night they flip and scamper on the dining and school-room floors where crumbs are left; even in the daytime they are in the kitchen and larder. Mrs Proutie, bending double with difficulty, her crinoline billowing behind her, her breath short, baits a trap and puts it down. There is a crack-snap of whale-bone. 'Nellie! Nellie! Help,' she cries to the kitchen maid. 'Oh Lord, my girl! Look 'ere. The 'ole thing 'as sat!' A mouse discovers the secret biscuit jar in the cupboard beside Selina's bed; it whisks away with crumb after crumb in front of the sleeping, snoring, flat pugnacious pug nose of Juno. The cat Gregory is a mouser; brief as the spells of his reign are, there are few mice left after them; fortunately for the mice, Gregory, like Richard Cœur de Lion, is almost always abroad on his crusades. Mouser the kitchen cat was misnamed; he would not mouse; he was too well fed. It makes no difference. There will always be plenty of mice.

In the study, the Eye and Griselda are discussing where to go for their summer holiday. Every year they discuss this and every year they go to Scotland.

'Couldn't we go right away, far away?' says Griselda. 'Think of going to China – or to Mexico!'

'My dear,' says the Eye, 'we are discussing a three weeks' holiday, not a voyage to the moon. Besides, I want to fish.'

'Yes John,' says Griselda. 'Yes,' she says slowly. 'Yes – of course.'

The Eye is watching her, a teasing light in his eyes. 'If we could go, even if we could go,' he asks her, 'you would not leave the children? Or would you? Would you, Griselda?'

She knows that he is teasing her, but, as with all his teasing, it holds hard grains of what ought to be the truth. 'You would not leave the children?'

Oh, but I would! cries Griselda but she does not say it aloud. It must be wrong, it is wrong, not to care for your children; not to want to see them and be with them and nurse them and play with them. 'You ought not to laugh John,' says Griselda very seriously. 'It ought to shock you.'

'But it doesn't,' says the Eye and he takes her by the elbows as she stands in front of him and sways her gently to and fro.

'Don't John dear,' says Griselda. 'It is wrong, very wrong not to care for your own little children. I don't understand it. Some day I shall be punished for it.'

'Oh, my darling love!'

'I wish, I wish I could feel differently about them.'

'We will have some more and perhaps you will like them better.' The Eye says it lightly but he is not altogether teasing, and her eyes go to his face quickly.

'You have the girl you wanted,' says Griselda slowly. 'You have Selina. We have six children.'

'Nine is my lucky number,' says the Eye.

Griselda suddenly turns away from him, so quickly that she catches her hoop on the corner of the writing table. She walks away to the window where he cannot see her face and the plane-tree throws its shade across the window. You will kill me with those great lumps of children. That is what she would like to fling at him, hateful coarse horrible words, but she remains silent, gazing, gazing at the plane-tree with hot eyes.

'Griselda dear.'

'I am sorry John.' And then she says slowly, 'You will be shocked John, I don't think I should have married. Perhaps – I am not a womanly woman.'

'And I think of you as the most womanly woman I have known.'

I might have married an explorer, thinks Griselda, looking at the cool branches of the plane-tree. I might have been an explorer myself. She sees herself returning from peculiar faraway shores in a ship that has a cargo of little precious many-coloured birds. But why returning? she asks herself. Why returning? Why not setting out? In a ship, a sailing ship, with the canvas bent into domes of white against a windy sky and an oily dangerous sea. The more dangerous the better. I have never seen a dangerous sea, thinks Griselda. Nor humming birds, nor a volcano. I have never seen, in the flesh, a Chinaman or an Indian, scarcely a foreigner but Fräuleins and Mademoiselles – and organ-grinders of course. I have seen musicians on concert platforms, but they were usually from far off. I have never seen a palm growing, says Griselda with the concert platform still in her eye. I have seen them at Torquay but that, says Griselda despising them, is like eating those drums of queer fruit that John brings back from the office, eating lichees and persimmons in our own dining-room. I should like, says Griselda, never to see our dining-room again.

As she says that, the house seems to reproach her. She turns her head and now she can look through the door, which is open, from the Eye's province to her own. Looking round her she sees the study, the long-shaped room, light resting on the books along the shelves making their colours soft and infinitely rich as if they were the colours of the infinitely wise. But no one, says Griselda to herself, can be wise for everyone. She moves towards the door and now she sees the window behind the Eye's chair and his head that is at the moment bent over a guidebook of Wales; the curtains hang in straight crimson lines, and the window-glass is marked with waterings of green, as watered ribbon is marked, by the branches outside. Back the other way through the door, the hall is dim, but the flowers on the stair-carpet show, and the air is full of those tiny tickings from the clocks, faint sounds from the nursery, faint sounds from the road, and an aroma of hot pastry and more sounds rising up the base-ment stairs. It is, however angry I am, it is, it is, my home.

'But – I should like to have gone all over the world first,' cries Griselda aloud.

'A house,' says the Eye looking up, showing that he has been following, not the guidebook, but his wife, 'a house can be the world. A whole universe. A whole world.'

'A tiny world for a woman,' answers Griselda hardly. 'A woman's world.'

'I think I have spoiled you, my dearest,' says the Eye.

You have, but not in the way you mean, she says, but she does not say it aloud, and silently too she says: You have never seen me. Not I who am Griselda. I should like never to see the dining-room again, says that Griselda. I should like to eat dates with – with the Arabs in the desert. White sand; white robes; white quivering sun; and quivering lusty netted Arab horses. I want to see prairies, empty of everything but grass: grass and wind, and is it bandicoots? Or simply, prairie dogs?

'You have never known me,' says Griselda to the Eye. 'You have never known what I am, what I could be. All you want and are determined to have is – an angel in the house.'

'I think,' said the Eye, 'that an angel would remember after eleven years that I don't take sugar in my coffee, and that I do like my socks to be darned and that someone should see to my handkerchiefs.' He holds up a tattered one to show her.

But Griselda does not look or feel remorseful. 'Can't you take me seriously?' she asks and her dark eyes are darker with anger. 'I believe you give more respect, John, to the few words a man in the street might say to you, than you do to me when I speak to you with my whole heart. But dolls don't have hearts do they?' says Griselda. 'Nor children? At least not hearts that are big enough to care.'

'There has been enough of this Griselda,' says the Eye sternly. He can be very stern.

Griselda is too angry to heed. 'You will grow larger and larger, and I shall grow smaller and smaller and we shall fill the house with more and more children, and it will begin all over again. I called you the Eye,' she says, 'because I thought you knew everything, saw everything, but I was wrong. It still suits you, because,' she flings at him, 'because you have only one eye – for yourselves – for all the Eyes in the world, the lords of creation, the race apart.'

'Griselda!'

'But be careful,' says Griselda. 'Be careful. Women have hearts and feelings even if you are careless of them. Be careful how you are careless John. You will hurt yourself one day.'

She turns her back on him and dabs her eyes with her handkerchief, but now her eyes are streaming and it is inadequate. The Eye silently gives her his torn one. She looks at it, and the tears come faster and faster.

'John, you are too good to me,' she whispers. 'Too good, and too patient. Far too patient. Why do you let me say things like this? I am a shocking wife.'

The Eye holds her in his arms, gently, firmly, and from his comfort it gradually comes to her that he is hardly even ruffled by the storm that has shaken her. The tears dry, she looks up at him with a strange almost calculatingly questioning look in her eyes.

'Well now,' says the Eye, 'we had better get back to our plans.'

'John, couldn't we go to Rome?'

'But—' says the Eye. 'I couldn't fish in Rome.'

It is Sunday morning.

Sunday morning in Wiltshire Place is distinguished by its quiet. The bells sound from St Benedict's with all the other London bells, an oranges and lemons chorus that begins before nine o'clock and continues until mid-morning and rings out again at evening into the quiet air.

The Place is extra quiet; carriages and cabs driven to the church stop at the west door in the Square, but all morning a gentle traffic goes on between the houses in the Place and the iron gate in the railings opposite. There are first a few, a very few in those days, who go to the early services which the new-fangled Vicar holds at eight and a quarter to nine; a few bonnets and shawls and a very few hats go over in the first chill winter daylight, often while the street lamps are being put out, the lamplighter running up to each of them to pull its chain and going on to the next lamp with his ladder on his shoulder; in summer, these few stop on their front steps to lift their faces to feel the promise of a day on which it seems a shame to leave the sparrows and the fugitive early freshness and go into the church. In pomp at eleven o'clock comes Matins, morning service. The enclosure round the church is filled; whole family groups, marshalled with sons and daughters, grown-up sons and daughters, schoolboys and girls, little sons and daughters, governesses and tutors, nurses, go in at the church door. There are uncles and aunts; young married couples; children, but if they are under five they will go out before the sermon. There are bachelors, young and old, and there are single ladies but these are always elderly unless they are not solitarily single, but attached to a father or mother or an aunt or a married brother or sister. The nuns come with their orphans; some are in the choir and the rest have pews of their own in the side aisles; they are all in uniform; Harry Proutie wears it; short black gowns for the boys and brown dresses, black aprons and starched white bonnets for the girls. The vergers sweep down the aisles in their black cassocks, their sashes swinging, and one opens and shuts a door giving a glimpse of the choirboys' starched whiteness and glossy brilliantined heads. The verger quite often cuffs one of those heads. There are figures that are familiar year after year though the Danes never know their names; there are the family with the brown eyes and the hats with cherries in them for instance; there are the old sisters with the hyacinth-coloured dresses, silk in summer merino in winter, and black bonnets and sealskin jackets and muffs; there is the man who comes alone and has such a rich baritone; these are figures year after year, Sunday after Sunday. There are others met here every week but who are friends, intimate since first they bowl their hoops with Pelham or with Selina towards the Basin, as the Round Pond is called then. Morning service is a public and a private ceremony and governs all the Sundays in the Place.

After it the Place is deserted, everyone has gone to church parade, all in their best Sunday clothes – in carriages if they have them; if not, to walk or sit on green-painted chairs on the green grass under the green trees, admiring the flowers, tulips or wallflowers or begonias, in the long beds, the very air feeling expensive and sanctified and gay.

At one o'clock the Place is quieter still; there is a long silence in which no front or back door opens and no face is seen at the windows; it is Sunday-dinner time. In every house great trays are carried up from the basement and on the trays are dishes with domes of metal covers, and the covers at Number 99 have black dolphins on the handles. A smell pervades the Place; the smell is chiefly of roast beef and Yorkshire pudding and roast potatoes cooked on a spit that turns on a brass cylinder with a cowl above it to keep in the steam and, below it, the roasting dish with the well for gravy, the potatoes and the pudding at the side, and the long-handled ladle to baste meat and pudding and potatoes to the same rich gravy brown. This is how Mrs Proutie cooks her roast. 'You don't get it to taste like that now,' complained Rolls. If it is not roast beef, it may be a saddle of mutton; or lamb and peas and spiced red-currant jelly; or capon; or a country chicken; or even, but this is rare, a sucking pig; Mrs Proutie lays the little pig out tenderly and garnishes it; she puts a little cut paper frill on the leg of lamb as it sticks up into the air from the dish in the rosy stains of its own sweet gravy; capon is not usual at Number 99, but she stuffs a chicken with her own secret stuffing and the kitchen is pungent with the smell of onion and herbs. The next course is almost universally apple tart and cream, but at Number 99 sometimes there may be trifle or plum duff. Then the heavy decanters, with their silver labels slung round their necks, are put on the table after the cloth is taken away; and nuts and the nutcrackers that are nearly as heavy as the decanters; and fruit on high fruit dishes standing on one slender fluted leg: muscatels, dried figs, or even a pineapple. After dinner on Sunday the children are allowed an orange.

The grown-ups rest after dinner and have a nap. At the foot of Griselda's bed is a couch and on the couch is a shawl kept folded, a Cashmere shawl that she is fond of for her shoulders, and an afghan for her feet; in the study there is a deep armchair; in Selina's room there is another armchair with blue and white chintz covers and a cushion. The children cross the Place again, for children's service. There are no bells to liven them and they silently fill the churchyard; small figures in pelisses and warm coats; buttoned boots; bonnets and Hussar caps, or Glengarrys; muffs and clean white gloves. The nurses have bonnets with veils; the governesses walk with tippets and prayerbooks; and black and brown and white come the colours of the orphans under the trees.

In the evening, at half-past five, the bells begin again, but they seem less tumultuous, more personal, in the evening; the sound of the bells of St Benedict's falls into the Square and the Place as if they rang for the Square and the Place alone. It is not obligatory to go to evening service, some go and some do not; some stay indoors and some take a gentle stroll; everything is gentle, a little flat, a little sad on these London Sunday evenings.

Griselda goes out, her hand on the Eye's arm; Selina crosses the Place and goes through the iron gate to the church where for the third time, the orphans, their faces bobbing pale in the dusk, go in by their special door below the Mary chapel. The sound of the organ comes out into the Place; the lamplighter comes back from the opposite direction leaving the lighted lamps gleaming in a line behind him; in the houses every moment a fresh window is lit up: the colours of stained glass shine crimson and jewel blue among the lime trees, from the church. Footsteps sound; voices gently call 'good night'; an area gate shuts and at a front door a house-owner stands and takes out his key. The organ sounds; they are singing the Nunc Dimittis preparatory to going home. *Lord, now lettest thou thy servant depart in peace according to thy word.*

Sunday is nearly over. There now remains only cold supper: cold beef and baked potatoes and a sodden English salad of lettuce and beetroot that tastes curiously of earth; cold pudding; a wine jelly with ratafia biscuits perhaps; more biscuits and cheese. Tea in the drawing-room and then leisurely, yawning, one by one to bed.

Now it is Sunday morning and in the drawing-room at Number 99 someone is practising her singing.

It is summer and the windows are open and the bowls, the Chinese thousand-flower-pattern bowls, hold yellow roses. Why do yellow roses smell more strongly than the other colours? The smell of these drowns the garden smell of lime-flowers.

> Ah – *ahahahahahah* – *ah*
> Ah – *ahahahahahah* – *ah* . . .

sings the voice.

> Ah – *ahahahahahah* – *ah*
> Ah – *ahahahahahah* – *ah* . . .

It changes to thirds: –

> Ah – *ah*
> Ah – *ah.*

It is Lark.

She is standing by the piano and the sun on the carpet reaches to her feet. She is wearing a dress of thin cream muslin that hangs in long fluted lines to the floor; it is tied at the waist and wrists and neck with old-gold ribbons, velvet ribbons of the new 'sunflower-gold'. This is one of the first dresses that have ever been made new for Lark; she has grown so tall that she can no longer wear Selina's cast-off dresses: Selina is tall but Lark is taller. The neck ribbon makes her neck look slight and rather long as it used to look when she was a child, but her hair is up, though she has not learned to cut it to a length that she can manage and it is a little uncertain and heavy and often tumbles down. Though she is so tall and her figure is magnificently full and rounded, she does not look quite adult; she is not: she has not yet emerged from the cocoon of quiet and separateness and shyness that distinguished her when she was a little girl. It is the same with her singing; each note is correct, full, even powerful, but she sends them out into the air as if she were not quite sure how they will sound.

She stands so still, so earnestly, that the folds of her dress might even be chiselled except that they fold down a little further when she bends to strike another note on the piano and take the scale up from it again: –

> Ah – ahahahahahah – ah
> Ah – ahahahahahah – ah . . .

Ascending and descending: –

> Ah – ahahahahahah – ah
> Ah – ahahahahahah – ah.

Then, sitting down at the piano, looking out across the garden, over the tops of the syringas to the limes, she begins to sing: –

> O Mary, go and call the cattle home,
> And call the cattle home,
> And call the cattle home,
> Across the sands of Dee!

The door opens so quietly that Lark does not hear it and Rollo stands there against the darkness of the hall.

Lark is usually only too much aware of Rollo when he is in the house.

The house becomes different; it is more alive: stirred, more interesting. His step rings in the hall; when he knocks he makes a tattoo with his cane on the panels of the front door; he laughs and Lark realizes how seldom it is that she, or Pelham or Selina, ever laughs. He has a way of calling for the servants instead of ringing that sounds cheerful and that they like. He brings in new elements; he plays cricket and no one else does; he rides and no one else does: he goes out in the evenings and comes in late; Lark sometimes hears him come in when it is first daylight and the sparrows in the nursery gutter – the nursery is now her bedroom – are cheeping. She hears him come upstairs and go past her door to his own room along the landing. He does not often come down to breakfast and Lark has caught glimpses of him, in a dark red dressing-gown eating kidneys on toast from a tray and talking to Slater. He does not often come down to breakfast but neither is he often in to lunch; nor does he have tea with Selina though she only sees him when he is on leave, nor does he dine at home. He seems, Lark thinks, to eschew the house as much as possible while he is on leave.

Rollo could have told her that the house to him seems gloomy and boring; there is nothing in his home, he thinks, to interest him. Selina spoils him, if he will let her bully him; Pelham spoils him but cannot help grudging it; Rollo quietly and consistently spoils himself and does not feel he need force himself to spend much time at home however short his leave.

'Look what I have done for you,' cries Selina.

'And how you did enjoy having someone to order about,' Rollo might have answered.

'Look what I do for you,' says Pelham.

'But you would really much rather do nothing at all.'

It has not occurred to Rollo to notice Lark.

Because of her old intimacy with Roly, Lark is shy of Rollo.

She keeps far out of his way but she knows almost as much about him as she knew about Roly.

His clothes for instance: they are quite different from Pelham's. Rollo has uniforms; of course Pelham cannot be expected to have those but Rollo has a cloak lined with white watered silk, Rollo has gardenias waiting on his dressing table and he chooses one when he has dressed. Lark sees Proutie putting studs into Rollo's evening shirts and Rollo has the magnificent diamond and ruby stud left him by the Eye. Rollo has rows of boots standing to attention with their trees. 'Can't he get boots in Worcestershire?' she hears Pelham say. On Rollo's dressing table are flasks, wicker-covered, silver-stopped, of cologne and bay rum and macassar oil; his hairbrushes, his handkerchiefs, even his pillow smell of them. In the corners of his mirror he puts invitation cards: *Lady Emily Chase – Mr and Mrs Henniker Grey*; notes are left open: *Dear Mr Dane – Lt R. I. Dane – Dear Rollo – Rollo dear, I wonder* ... There are programmes, gilded, with miniature pencils, pale-blue or pink or green or white or scarlet: –

No. 1 VALSE. MYOSOTIS. (*Barbara S.*)

No. 2 POLKA. TWO AND TURN AGAIN. (*Blonde curls. Under entrance palm.*)

No. 3 VALSE. DOWN THE RIVER OF YEARS. (*Blonde. Middle parting.*)

No. 5 BARN DANCE. (*Mary B. de V.*)

No. 6 VALSE. SEE SAW. (*Brown Eyes?*)

And Lark with a pang reads No. 7, No. 8, No. 11 and No. 12, No. 15, and No. 16: (*Brown Eyes?*). Sometimes the programmes have notes on them in Rollo's writing; sometimes the writing is someone else's: *St James 3* P.M., *Danvers 10:30*. Who – with that pang of envy – is Brown Eyes? Who, male or female, beautiful or hideous, sought or seeking, is Danvers?

There is, to add fuel to Lark's secret fire, much talk just now of Rollo in the house. She knows his shortcomings that Selina takes so seriously, and she knows his successes that Selina takes more seriously still. Now he has been transferred to the Indian Army, to the —th Punjab Cavalry. 'Better pay. Better promotion. Better prospects,' says Pelham. But ... and at last Lark, unable to bear it, has to point out, '*But* he will have to go to India!'

This vista, so appallingly open to her and to which they seem to blind themselves – 'Better pay. Better promotion. Better prospects' – is now close. In the autumn Rollo will sail for India.

'But how does this fit in with your ideas ... and Uncle Bunny's?' asks Pelham of Selina. 'Isn't it a step down?'

'A step down for several steps up,' says Selina and smiles.

'And he agrees?'

'Of course he agrees.'

Rollo agrees easily. 'Oh, all right,' says Rollo, 'but you must let me play polo this summer.'

'Polo!' Pelham pulls his upper lip. 'Polo is fabulously expensive.'

'Nonsense. Expensive but not fabulous. If you are wise,' says Selina, 'you will let him play polo.'

As May opens, and June, Selina in flowered dresses and delightful little tilted flower hats drives down to Ranelagh to watch Rollo play. I should wear hats like that, thinks Lark. I should be wearing them and not Selina. I shall ask Pelham if I can have a hat like that. I shall ask Pelham if I can go to

Ranelagh. But, in all she asks Pelham, she cannot bring herself to ask him that, and so the summer goes on and she and Rollo have not seen each other yet.

In spite of the fabulous polo and the qualities Lark and Selina weave round him, Rollo is truthfully a presentable but not extraordinary young man. He is not a swan but neither is he a goose. He has not grown up as good-looking nor as clever as Selina hoped, but then that was not likely nor, barely, possible. He is very big, very good-natured, and averagely quick-minded; he has a big strong healthy body, sunburned cheeks, Griselda's chestnut hair and blue eyes that are lazy and even-tempered and easily amused. He has, as well, the Eye's high forehead and Griselda's straight nose and something of her straight direct gaze. Rollo is not quite so lazy nor so even as he seems; he is ambitious and he has the Dane way of trenching deeply, leaving nothing undone that might help him in his career; but with this he is moody and he seems to turn even against himself as if he despises this ambition. 'Why do you do it?' asks Pelham. 'Don't you care about your work?' Rollo does care deeply but he still behaves as if he did not. 'He is so wild!' moans Selina. 'He won't go to church. He has such undesirable friends.' 'Why do you want to behave in such a worthless way?' asks Pelham.

'Perhaps because I don't believe very much in worth,' Rollo answers slowly.

'Why are you so discontented? No one forced you to go into the Army.'

'Didn't they?'

'You could have come into the business.'

'Business! What does anyone ever get out of business except a packet of money?'

'Well what do you want out of life?'

'Life.' Rollo might have answered that quite simply but he does not. He feels it, in moods that fluctuate; he feels it deeply but he is looking for words far more elaborate than that. Rollo once wrote poetry but he discovered quite soon that he was not a poet. I am not a poet but I know what a poet feels like. Even now, when according to Pelham and Selina he has settled down so nicely and become so sensible, still he knows. He has, like Pelham, a nostalgia but unlike most nostalgias, unlike Pelham's, it has power, a power of vision and penetration. He inherits it, as well as from Griselda, from the Eye; it is in the Eye's yearning after Griselda and the mother of Lark, after rubies and warm colours, and it is in Griselda's vision and her love of foreign words and things. For Rollo it is usually in words: in a sentence; in a play or in a poem; but it may also be in a winter morning: in a colour; the movement of leaves; an animal. It has not yet for him been found in a human, though once or twice he has thought ... Lark was right to feel that pang; Rollo was very much smitten with (*Brown Eyes?*), but she turns out to be only Brown Eyes without the (?) and he loses interest.

This morning Rollo is in evening dress and a little dishevelled; he has not taken off his hat and it is not on quite straight. Slater opens the door to him and Slater notices, and remarks downstairs, that Mr Rollo's breath was fruity. Rollo is not drunk, he is only elated. Now he stands in the doorway, listening to Lark. The room is full of light and sun and flowers; he blinks a little in the light and listens quietly.

The western wind was wild and dank with foam,
And all alone went she.

Lark is turned slightly away from him, singing towards the window; and Rollo, looking to where she is looking, to the green outside, seems to see a garden; it is another garden, not a London one; it is another garden of trees and groves and a stream with swans perhaps, but the swans are not white, they are black with scarlet bills. It is a poetical garden; the trees are weeping willow trees; there are old stone steps; a pedestal; it is a poetical garden but it is real. It is extraordinarily real. Now Rollo sees a dog, a bounding large curly-coated dog, and with him Lark is wandering, not singing now but walking, in just such trailing feminine skirts and, swinging by its loop of ribbon, a great garden hat. Lark? says Rollo to himself incredulously because he has not noticed or thought about the little girl enough to realize that one day she must grow into a woman; and then, with another shock, he sees Lark, not in any garden, but as she is now. He watches her at the piano and he sees the line of her face turned away from him, the too heavy dark hair, the sunflower ribbons. He has in this moment a perception of Lark; if he had not come at this moment he sees, he would not have seen her ever again as she is now. Women grow in minutes, not in years, thinks Rollo. Yesterday she was a child; to-morrow she will be complete, a woman. And as surely as Pelham saw, as Selina all these years has seen, Rollo, who is more fastidious and discerning, sees that she is beautiful. He sees, as well, how much more beautiful she will grow to be as she matures. He does not think of nymphs and goddesses; he thinks of himself. He is surprised at the feeling that has started up in him. She sings on unconsciously and in her singing is, he finds, his vision of the garden and the groves, the garden hat, the dog, the stream, the red-billed swans.

Across the sands of Dee!

There is a *ping*, a chime from the singing crystal in the chandelier.

The front door opens and shuts with a slam, quick steps cross the hall with a swishing of flounces, and Selina brushes past Rollo in the door.

'Lark!' she calls peremptorily. 'Lark.'

'Hush,' says Rollo angrily but the song breaks off abruptly and with her hands still on the keys Lark swings round with startled eyes. Then she sees Rollo.

'Lark! Have you forgotten it is Sunday?'

'Sunday?' says Lark vaguely. She barely hears Selina. She is looking at Rollo and the colour in her cheeks deepens, pales, deepens more vividly again. Rollo comes into the room.

'Take off your hat,' says Selina to Rollo, and to Lark: 'They could hear you at the end of the road. Right down the Place.'

Lark does not listen but Rollo has obediently taken off his hat.

'I am speaking to you Lark.'

'I thought you were at church,' Lark says absently.

Rollo has come up to her, leaning on the piano lid, close to the bowl of roses that Selina insists on putting on the case, with a draped Indian shawl and a water colour on a miniature easel. The scent of the roses is heavy and strong.

Selina has now to speak to Lark past Rollo's back and he seems to intercept her words so well that they do not reach Lark. 'You thought I had gone to church. I had but I had to come back for a handkerchief. So this is how you behave as soon as my back is turned. You were positively shouting. What will everyone think?'

'They will think that Sunday morning in Wiltshire Place has lost a little of its depression and repression and gloom,' says Rollo turning round on her. 'Its gloom and its smugness and hyp-hyp-hypocritical humbug.' He turns back again to Lark across the yellow roses and says softly to her, 'I know now why they called you Lark.'

She answers still more softly, 'Were you there, listening all the time?'

Selina has been looking more closely, very closely, at Rollo. 'Rollo! Are you going out, like *that*?'

'I am not going out. I am c-coming in. I am on my way to bed.'

'At this time of the morning?' She looks at him again and comes closer and recoils. 'Rollo! Your breath! You smell of wine and spirits – terribly.'

'I have been drinking them,' says Rollo reasonably. 'Don't fuss Lena. I am not drunk.'

Lark has noticed his breath but she does not mind it. It smells rather like raisins and is, she thinks, a little exciting, but Selina is angry. 'You should go to your room, not appear before ladies, before me or a young girl. Take no notice of him Lark. It is too much!'

'Don't fuss Lena,' says Rollo.

'Fuss! I shall speak to Pelham, but Pelham takes no more notice than a sheep. I shall speak to Uncle Bunny. He will deal with you.'

'Don't fuss Lena,' says Rollo patiently. He still smiles but his eyes are not amused. The bells for morning service stop their ringing and a fresh thought strikes Selina.

'Rollo! You must have met everyone on their way to church!'

'I d-did.'

'Oh – *No!* What *did* you do?'

'I l-lifted my hat and said "G-good night,"' says Rollo gravely.

Lark laughs an infectious rich peal in the room and Rollo begins to laugh too. 'This isn't funny,' cries Selina. 'It is perfectly disgusting. What will people think? What will they say!'

Then Selina thinks of something else. Lark sees her face change, her eyes go rapidly over Rollo summing him up; a possibility has occurred to her. 'Well,' she says and now her voice has altered, it is coaxing, only a little hurried. 'Oh well. I suppose it is no use being cross with you Rollo. But you must be punished.'

What does she want, thinks Lark. What is she after?

'You must go straight upstairs and change. I shall ring for Proutie to help you. You must be quick, change in five minutes, and then you must come over with me to church.'

'You will be very late,' says Lark idly. 'The bells have stopped.'

'Be quiet,' hisses Selina. 'You will do that for me, won't you Rollo?'

'No I won't,' says Rollo.

'Rollo please. To please me.'

'No.'

'Rollo dear.'

'But why do you want me to Lena?'

Because, Lark could have told him, because if you appear in church with her, groomed and respectable, it will perfectly correct the scandal of your appearance in the Place this morning. That is what Selina in her mind is saying. Lark could have told him. That is what is in her mind. But Lark does not say anything. She watches to see what Rollo will do.

Rollo will not go to church. That is one of the most discussed points of his behaviour. He will not go. On principle he will not go. Lark waits to see what he will do.

'You know I won't go to church,' growls Rollo.

'You go to Church Parade.'

'That is because of the men.'

'If you go because of your men, won't you go for your own sister?'

'No I won't,' says Rollo again, and he says – uncomfortably because he is not given to explaining himself – 'I don't believe in it Lena. I won't hurt you by saying what I think, but I don't believe in it. You know I don't.' He is, Lark sees, uncomfortable; nothing deeper.

Selina brushes his words away as if they were flies. 'That doesn't matter,' she says.

Doesn't matter at all, says a cool small voice somewhere inside Lark. Appearances matter. As long as you appear to believe it doesn't matter what you believe. Will you consent to appear Rollo? Will you lie? And she looks at Rollo's face that is sulky but not stiff with obstinacy as she would have liked to see it. Oh well ... most people lie, thinks Lark.

'To please me, Rollo.'

'Oh very well!'

'Dear dear naughty boy!' says Selina delighted. 'Thank you. Thank you.' She kisses him and her veil tickles his cheek and irritates him. 'Dear boy! I shall go and tell Proutie to put out your clothes and help you; but you must hurry. Hurry!'

She goes out quickly. Rollo lingers. There is a silence. Lark says nothing. She looks at her hands on the silent piano keys. She presses one down softly and it gives out the shade of a note, and a shade answers it from the crystal. Then the room is quite silent, fragrant and full of sun.

'It is no use defying Selina,' says Rollo defensively.

'It is of use,' says Lark. 'And you are free of them,' she points out.

'I am not. I can't live on my pay.'

'You could.'

He could. He knows that. 'And I hate asking Pelham for money.' He does not realize that he has said that aloud.

'Then why do you?'

'Because he always has some and will always give some of it to me,' he says disarmingly, but she does not smile. 'Once—' says Rollo and stops. He seems lifted by a feeling of freedom, as if with Lark freedom would come. 'Once I asked him to give me five hundred pounds and let me go,' says Rollo.

'If I had money,' says Lark thoughtfully, 'I would give you five hundred pounds.'

'But I wouldn't go now for that,' says Rollo laughing; he has withdrawn. Then he sees the garden again; Lark's skirts; her dark hair . . . the birch-green ribbon, the pale chip straw of the hat. 'Do you know that you are beautiful? Beautiful?' he says.

'Rollo! What are you doing? We must be quick. Be quick Rollo *dear*!' and Selina sweeps between them into the room.

At half-past eleven Proutie came upstairs again.

'Miss Grizel, I am sorry to disturb you but a young officer has called.' He held out a salver with a card. 'Pilot Officer Masterson, miss. He asked to see Mr Rolls, but Mr Rolls is in the study and gave strict orders that he was not to be disturbed. He gets so upset if I go in and I daren't disturb him, but it seems the gentleman has a very special message. Would you see him Miss Grizel?'

'Of course Proutie. Show him up here.'

Proutie went down and came up with a small dark-skinned young man in uniform. He had, Grizel noticed, as he crossed the landing, his right arm in a sling and his hand in bandages. She stood up to meet him.

'My great-uncle is busy,' she said. 'Can you talk to me instead? I am Grizel Dane.'

He gave her a quick look of surprise and took her hand as if he did not know he held it. 'But how do you fit in?' he said. 'I haven't heard of you. You don't belong here, do you?'

'But I do,' said Grizel surprised.

He gently released her hand. 'I didn't mean to be rude. I'm sorry. Can I explain?'

'Come and sit down,' said Grizel. She led the way to the window-seat but he did not sit down. He stood looking round him. Grizel watched him curiously. As he turned, looking intently, he moved in and out of the light, and that changed him and altered him and impressed him on Grizel. He was unusually dark, with an olive southern-looking skin, jet-dark hair, black eyes; his uniform made him look darker still, the blue bringing out the greenishness in his skin. It doesn't become him, thought Grizel. I had thought it became everyone.

What was he saying? 'I remember the geography,' he said, and he looked at the doors. 'There is Mrs Dane's, Griselda's, room. That is the dressing-room, and that room is Selina's.'

'Now it is mine.'

'And do you drive Selina out? I bet you don't. She was a dragon, wasn't she? And,' he added gravely, 'she was unkind.'

'She doesn't worry me,' said Grizel. 'I don't think I have much sense of the past, or of history, or of family. I like the present. I like people – not ancestors.'

'Ancestors are people,' he answered and he studied her. 'You are a Dane. How do you manage to be an American?'

'I was born one,' said Grizel. 'My grandfather, Pelham Dane, went to America to be married in eighteen ninety-one.'

'And you have no sense of the past?' he asked. 'Then why did you come back here?'

'What has that to do with it? I didn't come here for the past. If I came for anything,' said Grizel, 'I suppose it was for the future. Yes, it has always seemed to me more sensible to think of the future. The past has gone.'

'Has it?'

'Of course it has. It is over. Done with. What are you smiling at?'

'You,' he said.

'At me?'

'Yes. You are so glib.'

'*Glib?*' Grizel could not say more for her astonishment.

'It must be wonderful,' he said, 'to be able to divide everything up separately and label it so certainly and put it away in such air-tight, thought-proof boxes.'

'What makes you think I have – *boxes?*'

'Haven't you? This is the past. I am not interested in the past. Shut it up, put it away. This is the future. We should think of that. Better keep it open.' And he said rudely: 'What about the present? Where does that begin and end? I suppose you know that too?'

'You are very rude,' said Grizel. 'I think—'

'You don't,' he said. 'You don't think.' His face softened as he looked at her. 'Probably you won't think. Try it. Try thinking,' he suggested.

'Pilot Officer Masterson,' said Grizel. 'You have known me five minutes—'

'And nothing can happen in five minutes?' He stopped and there was silence and then he came closer to her and said, looking out over her head as she sat on the window-seat, 'Again I am sorry. I don't know how this argument began. I came here in a perfectly normal state of mind. I don't usually beard people like this.' Grizel did not speak. 'I am stationed at Hornchurch,' he said, 'and we have had a bit of a party these months. I suppose it is that and I am not quite normal. It was a strain; people not coming in and the waiting all the time. Then I got my unlucky shot.'

'You crashed?'

'Yes, off Margate. Slap into the drink. Fortunately for me the lifeboat people saw me come down. I was back at the aerodrome in a few hours. All I got was this.' He showed his hand. 'Burnt. I have to have an operation but they say I shall use it in a fortnight.'

'Don't!' said Grizel, more sharply than she meant. She stood up beside him, looking down into the Place, empty in a cold grey winter morning, with the steeple coldly clearly grey in the daylight and the brass balls of the weathercock shining. All ordinary, commonplace, everyday, like any other winter morning in any time except – Except for what? Not something so different in it, different as it was, but something different in Grizel. 'I get horrors over this war,' said Grizel slowly. 'Sometimes I don't think I can bear it. I don't think I am very good at going on being brave.'

'Why didn't you stay in America? Why are you here?'

'That is my business,' said Grizel and there was a different tone in her voice, a shyness.

'It is your business,' he answered her. 'Your business. My business. Everyone's business. I don't think anyone is meant to escape this time.' And he added, 'It wasn't so easy for me. I am half-Italian.'

'That must have been hard,' said Grizel.

'It continues to be hard,' he said lightly and Grizel thought that he spoke particularly lightly when he was particularly moved. 'The mechanics were easy. I was in the R.A.F. in 'thirty-six. My father was English you see. The mechanics were easy but it was not easy. My childhood was spent in Italy. I was brought up there by my uncle because I was his heir. He had rather large estates. There were things I had to learn. He was the Marchese Zacca del Laudi. He is dead now.'

'Then –' said Grizel – 'besides being Pilot Officer Masterson you are the Marchese – I can't remember the rest.'

'I am both of them,' he said. 'That is it. But I am Pax, myself, as well.'

'And you know this house. When were you here?'

'I was never here.'

'But you *know* it.'

'The Marchesa, my uncle's wife, was English. She lived in this house as a child, and as a girl. She and I were very dear to one another. She used to play a game with me, hide and seek all over this house.'

'But you said—'

'Oh, we were not here. Neither of us. I think she was home-sick, there was something that seemed always – continually to be in her thoughts. She taught me the house from top to bottom. I could show you your way in it I think.' He laughed. 'She used to make me fly upstairs. Even then I used to think of flying. That made the game perfect for me. I always flew upstairs.'

'Where is she?' asked Grizel.

'In Italy. I don't suppose anything would happen to her,' he said again lightly, 'she has been there among the people for too long. No, she will be down at Laudi in Tuscany. That was the country home of ours that she loved and I left it to her to live in. She made a garden there, a famous one. I think she had almost forgotten this house, until lately.'

'Lately?'

He turned away from the window looking down at Grizel and his eyes seemed very small and bright as Grizel was to learn they looked when he was earnest. 'I haven't seen her for two years,' he said slowly. 'I haven't perhaps thought of her very much, or felt the thought of her, but lately it is as if she has been nagging me to come here. No, not nagging, reminding; reminding, continually reminding me. Don't laugh at me,' he said to Grizel. 'She told me to come here and I came.' And he asked her: 'Where is General Dane? Where is – Rollo?'

'I called him that,' said Grizel, 'and he said "Rollo was my name when I was young. Only one person calls me that."'

'She has not seen him for fifty years,' said Pax, objecting.

'But it might not have been your aunt, the Marchesa, who calls him that,' said Grizel. 'Why do you take it for granted?' Then she added, puzzled, 'But it isn't "Why do you take it for granted?" It feels more like "What do you take for granted?"'

'There is something, isn't there?' said Pax.

'It seems authentic,' admitted Grizel. 'He shuts himself away by himself, but it is not to be unhappy. He isn't unhappy. He seems to be finding some happiness, some joy of his own. What was her name? Your aunt, what was her name?'

'Her name is Lark.'

As he said that, a sound made them turn. Rolls had come upstairs and stood at the top of the flight by the banisters resting for a moment.

He did not look at all like an old gentleman shut away to brood inside his study with the door closed against them all. He looked singularly hale and cheerful. Not a blood, not a blood but a blade. 'Hullo,' he said to Grizel. 'Do you sit here too? This has always been where the women of the family like to sit.'

He crossed to her. He did not appear to see Pax standing full in his way in the window.

'Uncle Rolls,' Grizel began, 'this is Pilot Officer—'

Rolls interrupted her. 'I come here to look at the snow,' he said.

'Snow?'

'They used to tell us,' said Rolls and chuckled, 'that it was the angels airing their pillows: goose feathers. Geese!' He peered out past Grizel. 'And the men with drays put sacks on their shoulders and heads, and if it were bad they put gravel down to stop the horses slipping.'

'But Uncle Rolls—' said Grizel.

Pax made a gesture to her to be quiet. It was such an instinctive commanding authoritative rightful gesture that Grizel stopped and was quiet, looking at him. Then she flushed and said again, deliberately: 'Uncle Rolls—'

'I don't see it lie as it used to do,' Rolls complained. 'Heavy pure snow, and the air was pure too even here in London. That is what I liked. But never mind, even now I like to see it coming quietly down.'

'But Uncle Rolls, it is winter,' cried Grizel, 'it is winter but it hasn't snowed yet.'

FOUR O'CLOCK

It was four o'clock and on the landing Pax was having tea with Grizel. It was ten days since Pax had come into the house, ten days that had passed with wings and to-morrow was the eleventh of December when Proutie was to start packing and Grizel and Rolls were to leave the house.

'Have you packed?'

'No-o,' said Grizel slowly. 'I still can't believe we are going. And if I can't,' she said, 'after being here three weeks, what must it feel like for Uncle Rolls?'

It had turned colder and already the afternoon was growing dusk; outside the window the light was grey and presently, in the twilight, it began to snow. Grizel turned her head and watched the flakes coming down. Angels airing their pillows. That was what Rolls had said. People believed in angels then. I wish I did, said Grizel. I wish I could. I need an angel. I wish I had something to steady me: a hand to cling on to. Yes, I wish I had an angel.

Grizel was more than ever adrift and confused and she was

frightened. She was not accustomed to being anything but clear and firm, confirmed, and secure. That first night in London she had confessed to being rattled but it was more even than that. She had been shaken and continued to be shaken. And now nothing in me can settle. I am all unsettled. Why? Why? What is happening to me? She glanced across at Pax and away again. She refused utterly to think of him.

She had been a child like every other child; dependent: loving her mother and father; her nurse; she had made friendships at school and had school admirations – though perhaps mine were more temperate, lukewarm than most. I never burned, thought Grizel. She had been in love. In spite of that most firm refusal she found she was looking at Pax again and she knew, most certainly, that she had never been in love. I have been nearly in love then, corrected Grizel. Through all her life, through all these loves, she had remained herself, her entity, Grizel. *I am I because my little dog knows me* says Gertrude Stein; but I haven't any little dog, nor even an angel, said Grizel.

It was her work first she thought that had first disembodied her. She was just a unit in a unit, clothed in khaki, gauntleted, well-shod, pink-cheeked, efficient. Then, when she had finished work and came back to the house, what was left of her was infringed; Eroded, said Grizel indignantly and she said again bewildered, I am not I! It did not occur to her that, perhaps for the first time, she was learning what she really was: infinitesimal; a grain in the sand; the spring-off of her tribe; the continuation, nothing more, of what was gone; and now Pax had come and again she was looking at him, forcing herself to look away and at once looking back at him.

The landing, in the increasing dusk, was lit by the glow of

Proutie's electric fire, two opal and orange globes in a copper shield; the glow spread over the carpet, was thrown up to the edge of the white tablecloth, on to the chairs, and up the blue of Pax's trousers to his knees; it was reflected again in the silver of the tea-things, even in the strainer as Grizel lifted it, the strainer that Griselda uses every teatime.

The house is filled with possessions like the silver strainer with the silver primroses on the handle that match the tea-pot and hot-water jug, the milk jug, cream jug and sugar basin; there is a massive silver tray; the salvers; much silver and plate of the calibre of the grape-leaved entrée dishes; there is a set of spoons and forks, raft-tailed, worn fine, inherited by the Eye: there is the new set, so much more solid, ordered by him from Mappin and Webb; there are toast racks and butter dishes and jam spoons, and salt-cellars and mustard-pots and a little walnut barrel capped with silver for grinding peppercorns; there is an enormous cruet in a plated holder with eight cut-glass bottles; there are silver labels on the decanters and a set of tiny filigree holders for liqueur glasses; there are candelabra with six branches and a set of silver vases shaped like convolvulus with silver tendrils for the dinner table; there are all the christening mugs of course: a silver rattle and baby forks and spoons; there is a giant ladle of solid silver for soup and a delicate ladle with a tortoise-shell handle for punch. Tortoise-shell too is the tea-caddy on little silver legs; one of the first things Pelham and Selina remember is the little caddy standing on the tea-table above the lace and linen of the cloth and catching the firelight in its tortoise-shell sides, on just such winter afternoons.

There are six or seven tea-sets in the house, ranging from the plain white kitchen set with its odd pieces and the nursery set, at one time white too with violets, to the Davenport in the cabinet in the hall, in grey and white and gold. There is a doll's tea-set in Dresden china with an edging of china lace. The dinner service in everyday use is white with a border of royal blue and flowers in red and brown and gold: there is also a French set, a Limoges copy in white porcelain with scattered nosegays of flowers; there is a best set in white fluted china, plain, almost transparent, Spode. The dessert service used every day is hideous with dishes shaped like green china baskets, but there is a Worcester set, white again with a deep cherry border and centre flowers of gold; there are Chinese bowls, sent as presents sometimes to the Eye with his cargoes of tea; blue-and-white bowls with a rice pattern on them and blue-and-white lids; and the thousand-flower-pattern Chinese bowls in the drawing-room.

The Danes are proud of their glass, cut glass and plain heavy crystal; Selina buys a cocktail set in nineteen twenty-three, a set with red and black cocks on the glasses: Grizel equips the kitchen with Pyrex; but the Eye has a goblet with a George II florin embedded in a bubble in its base and Griselda has a precious set of Waterford given her for her wedding by Roly's godfather, whom afterwards they call Uncle Bunny.

Griselda's wedding linen far outlasts Griselda. Grizel cuts some of her ample double sheets into sheets for single beds and has the monogram unpicked and embroidered in again; the sheets are as good as new. Two huge presses on the second floor hold the linen that Griselda's mother thinks necessary for Griselda on her marriage; this is both added to and slightly denuded with the years; there are sheets and cot sheets, pillowcases, hemstitched and embroidered and edged with Limerick lace; there are sizes and sizes of bath towels and hand towels, and face towels with embroidered edges; there are huge damask tablecloths and large starched napkins to match; fragile tea-cloths, and there are Grizel's lace dinner mats with the petit-point centres; there are blankets stored away for the summer and dusters in dozens that the maids have to hem.

The Eye has a safe in his study for papers and another in his dressing-room where he keeps Griselda's jewellery. Griselda's jewels are good but not notable, but when Grizel inherits Lark's things sometimes the Laudi emeralds are there. There are the rubies the Eye gives Griselda: his own ruby-and-diamond dress stud; Griselda's sapphire engagement ring; the diamond brooch he gives her when Pelham is born and the brooches that follow, one for each child with each one's birth-day stone; there are seven brooches: the twins share and after Rollo Griselda does not need a brooch. There are the pearls that Rollo gave Lark. There is also, at times, with her other jewellery, Grizel's engagement ring, a cameo, of a cherub with pink wings.

On Griselda's left hand as she lifts the strainer is a wide plain gold band; on Grizel's left little finger that afternoon was a signet ring, the bird with a sheaf of wheat in its beak engraved on onyx, and the fire was reflected in it too. The glow had the effect of linking Pax and Grizel together; it warmed their cheeks and hands and shut them away in a circle by themselves, away from the shadowy depths of the staircase and the cold light beyond the window where the snowflakes fell. It gave them, at the tea-table, a feeling of intimacy.

But I don't want to be intimate with Pax, objected Grizel, and as if she were divided into two halves, one sterner than the other, she found herself asking herself, Then why did you ask him to tea?

On the evening of that first day Pax had written Grizel a long apology. You needn't have answered it, she told herself. If you wanted to be quit of him that was a crazy thing to do. And you went and had lunch with him next day and then you went and saw him in hospital. But I had to do that, argued the mild Grizel, that was common humanity. But not every day, snapped the other.

Pax was talking, '... And so they built me two fingers,' he was saying quite unaware and peacefully, 'out of a little piece of my thigh. McCullough says they will look quite normal when it has all grown in. The man in the next bed to me had new lids to his eyes. They graft the skin on. Sometimes you give yours for some-one else.'

'If I had to be done,' said Grizel, 'I should prefer it to be my own thigh.'

Pax laughed. 'Oh Grizel! What a funny little self-contained creature you are.'

'I was,' said Grizel slowly. But now I am not, and I wish, I wish, I were, she cried silently and she said aloud before she could check herself: 'I sometimes wonder if I contained anything else but self.'

Pax looked at her in surprise and she stood up and pushed back her chair and went to the window. He did not move. He asked gently from the firelight, 'What is wrong Grizel?'

She said after a moment, 'Pax, when you told me that they said they thought you would be all right, you meant all right for flying, didn't you?'

'Yes,' said Pax.

'I have seen planes all my life,' said Grizel to the snow. 'Seen them and travelled in them. I remember in New York looking up from our balcony at night and seeing them go over with their lights. On a clear night it looked as if the stars were loose. But of course you don't have lights.'

'No, we don't have any lights.'

'Are you ever frightened Pax?'

'I hope my particular fright won't happen to me,' he said. 'Possibly it may not. Probably it will. One day I may be sent out over Italy.'

'I hadn't thought of that,' Grizel turned round to him.

'I have,' said Pax and he went on steadily, looking at her. 'I have thought of Italy more lately; almost continually. I wonder if it is that, that has brought Lark so vividly to my mind.'

Don't talk about Lark now, Grizel wanted to say jealously, when you ... when I ...

'Laudi and Lark,' he went on. 'I don't think I have ever thought of them as vividly and realistically as I do now.' He looked at his hands, linked together in the firelight that lit the edges of them and made them look sensitive and thin. 'It is so vivid that I have wondered if anything could have happened. We arranged, if anything did, that I could be reached through Switzerland where my cousin, Arno, is working in the Red Cross, but of course news would take ages to come. I think of her so much,' said Pax. 'Before, I thought of her as a child thinks of a grown-up person, as we are apt to think of people we have known all our life; now I think of her as a man of a woman.' Grizel had another pang of jealousy and this time it was so sharp that it hurt her, and then Pax said, 'I think of her, and the thought is bound up in you.'

'In me?'

'Yes. You,' said Pax, looking at his hands.

'Pax,' Grizel had turned back quickly to the window, but she did not see the snow now, her eyes were fixed, deep with thought. 'Pax, after the flying, after the excitement and the power, does anything seem real or desirable any more to you?'

She did not have to wait for his answer; it was immediate and quite certain. 'Real? Desirable?' said Pax. 'The earth? I think it is.' He gave the four little words their full exact weight. 'More than ever,' said Pax, 'do I realize and desire,' and then he said, 'Grizel ...'

The dressing-room door opened and Rolls came out, brushed and combed and washed, his coat changed, a fresh handkerchief in his pocket. He looked perfectly cheerful and unperturbed.

'Here is Uncle Rolls,' said Grizel quickly. 'We must ask him to have some tea. It is our last day here you know and he must feel it terribly.'

'He doesn't look very disturbed,' said Pax.

'Well he ought to be,' snapped Grizel, and she called, 'Uncle Rolls, come and have some tea.'

Rolls looked from one of them to the other. Grizel thought he was going to refuse and she went to him and took his arm. 'I haven't seen you for days,' she said. 'Come and have tea with us. You remember Pax, Pilot Officer Masterson? He came to see us because of Lark.'

'Lark?' She thought a beam of light, a spark quivered in his eyes and she went on insistently. 'The Marchesa Zacca del Laudi. Pax is her nephew and he is the Marchese now. You remember him Uncle Rolls.'

'I remember,' said Rolls considering her. 'But why are you so excited? I hear you Grizel.'

'Have you done your packing?' asked Grizel leading him to the table.

'No,' said Rolls shortly.

Grizel poured out his tea, and filled Pax's cup. 'Pax,' she said, 'you talk so much about her, tell me what she is like.'

There was something intrusive and clamorous in her words. Pax looked across at Rolls and Rolls looked at Pax. There was a sympathy between them from which Grizel was shut out. 'Tell her,' said Rolls. 'Grizel, you asked me to tea and now you don't give me any tea.'

Grizel hastily passed him his cup and poured out another for herself. Her hand was shaking.

'You would think she was a very tall old lady,' said Pax to her, watching her gently with his eyes that looked small and bright. He put out a hand and pulled her down in her chair. 'Sit still Grizel.' He said: 'She is tall and – upright; yes, that is the word for her. Though she is old her figure is young, but her left hand has a perpetual little shake. She is vain and she tries to hide it by using a stick, a carved ebony stick, and she always holds it in that hand.' Rolls smiled. Grizel, watching him minutely, saw that smile.

'Her hair is white and she wears it high with combs,' Pax went on, 'and she wears earrings. She likes long earrings and she has exquisite filigree ones and they emphasize her eyes and the bones of her face. I told you she was vain.' Grizel saw Rolls, still with that smile, nod his head.

'Her eyes are startling,' said Pax. 'They always were?' he asked Rolls.

'They were startling memorable eyes,' said Rolls.

'I think they are even more noticeable now that her hair is

white,' said Pax. 'They are beautiful eyes,' he said to Grizel. 'They are blue, not true blue like yours, but half violet.'

'Are mine true blue?' asked Grizel, but Pax was still telling of Lark.

'She is quite all right, quite safe,' said Pax to Rolls. 'She is down at Laudi. She would have Ranulph with her. Ranulph is our St Bernard dog. She will see hardly anyone but Leonarda, Leonarda is her old maid, and Battiste Volpi. Battiste Volpi is the head gardener and he is devoted to her. She liked to be there alone in the garden. It is a green garden,' he explained to Grizel. 'It has a famous grove of willow trees, and it has a river and old marbles. She grew flowers there. She liked flowers more than people I often thought.'

'I wouldn't know,' said Rolls disagreeably. 'I haven't had time for flowers.'

Grizel looked at him in astonishment but Pax went on, 'Of course, I haven't seen her for two years.'

'I don't need to see her,' said Rolls and it sounded to Grizel as if he crowed over Pax, and looking at him she thought suddenly of the first day when he had touched her, turned up her chin to see her face and she remembered the warmth of his touch. Uncle Rolls, you are jealous! she said to herself and he looked up and met her look.

'Why don't you have a romance of your own?' he suggested kindly.

Grizel was immediately confused and half angry. 'I am – busy,' she said gruffly.

'You must be,' said Rolls gravely. 'She is the youngest officer in the whole corps,' he told Pax and his voice was half derisive and half proud. 'In my day you worked ten years and not ten minutes before you got promotion but, well – I expect they are proud of you,' he bantered Grizel.

'They are not,' cried Grizel hotly.

'What? Don't they like you, hey?'

'They call me "the Great Dane",' said Grizel.

'So they did me,' said Rolls chuckling. 'So they did me.'

'Pax, you ought to go,' said Grizel. 'Your appointment is at five.'

'Yes, I shall have to,' said Pax looking at his watch. 'I have to see my beauty doctor, sir, and get to Wimpole Street.' He looked at Grizel. 'Come with me?'

'No,' said Grizel.

'Yes,' said Pax, getting up.

She hesitated and then stood up too. Rolls's eyes were surveying them both. His eyes, she thought, looked extraordinarily tired. They seemed sunk in shadows.

'Proutie says you have been sitting up all night,' she said. 'While I have been on this late duty, you have been up all night. You shouldn't do it, Uncle Rolls.'

His eyes at once lost their dreaminess, they were no longer sunk; they glared. 'There is one rule in this house Grizel and you are going to keep it,' said Rolls glaring down at her, 'or even for this remaining night you can go. I don't wish to be disturbed, and I shall not be disturbed. Do you understand? You can sleep at the hotel.'

'This is my night off,' said Grizel looking straight back at him, 'but I shan't sleep at the hotel.'

'Wouldn't it be best,' said Pax, 'if you came out dancing with me?'

'No,' said Grizel.

'Yes,' said Pax.

Rolls smiled. 'I think that is a good idea,' he said. 'It will get you out of the way. But won't you come and dine here with us first?' he asked Pax. 'It is the last time I can ask you. Dine with me, but after dinner you must go out together and leave me in peace.'

'But won't you come?' asked Pax.

'Good God my God no!' said Rolls. 'I want to be left alone. The condition is that I am left alone.'

'I shall come back then, after the doctor,' said Pax. 'Thank you, sir. I shall have to ring up first. About eight? Come along Grizel.' He took her elbow to turn her to the stairs.

'Don't pull me about. I can go alone,' snapped Grizel but Pax took no notice. He led her to the top of the stairs.

'Get your coat,' he said. 'Be quick,' and Grizel went quietly into Selina's room. Rolls watched them; he watched Grizel come out with her coat and stand waiting for Pax; together they ran down the stairs. Rolls crossed the landing and went to the window and watched them go away down the Place.

'Rollo?' It was a whisper.

'Lark? We have been talking of you.' He plunged into his objection. 'You like that boy don't you?'

'And what about your little minx Grizel?' said the cool musical voice that always seemed for Rolls to make everything clear. 'You like her too.'

'I didn't at first, I do now. She seems necessary,' said Rolls.

'She is necessary,' said the Marchesa regretfully.

'You don't like her Lark?'

'She is a cold little fish. I hope she doesn't hurt my Pax. She is a Dane. Her head is stronger than her heart.'

'She is learning,' said Rolls. 'I don't think you are quite fair.' And he added, 'She is a pretty thing. That makes it easy for me to like her.'

'She isn't half as pretty as I was at her age. I was a beauty. You should have seen me my first winter in Rome.'

'I saw you,' said Rolls. 'Lark, those two, this afternoon . . . '

'Don't envy them,' said the Marchesa quickly. 'We mustn't envy them. It isn't safe.'

'But they still have their chance. We might have been so happy.'

'Hush,' said the Marchesa. 'What is the use of disturbing it? We are happy now.'

'All the same, I wish, I wish it were you who were dining with me to-night, really, actually, and not those two.' There was resentment in the way he continually said 'Those two.'

'My boy? Your girl? Don't be angry with them. They continue us and so they are us Rolls. I shall be dining with you to-night. Shall it be summer or winter?' asked the Marchesa. 'Shall we be in the dining-room with the peacock curtains drawn, and the candlelight shining on the table and the silver and the portrait frames? With the clock ticking, and a fire? And the comfortable smell of wine and soup and bread, and I believe you have a pheasant Rolls? And nuts and figs and raisins, and coffee afterwards? Or shall it be summer? Have you noticed,' she asked, 'that it is always winter at the front of the house and summer in the garden? Shall it be summer and after dinner you can go out on the balcony and smoke your cigar? But have you a cigar?'

'A private store – for occasions.'

'This is an occasion. And I shall sing for you. Now I smell lime-flowers Rolls.'

'Not lime-flowers, yellow roses,' said Rolls.

As Rolls stood there by the landing window, from far down below in the house there seemed to come the sound of singing; it sounded out into the garden and faintly up the stairs.

> *Ah – ahahahahahah – ah*
> *Ah – ahahahahahah – ah . . .*

Up the scale and down the scale: –

> *Ah – ahahahahahah – ah*
> *Ah – ahahahahahah – ah . . .*

In thirds: –

> *Ah – ah*
> *Ah – ah.*

And then rounding more clearly into a song: –

> *O Mary, go and call the cattle home,*
> *And call the cattle home,*
> *And call the cattle home,*
> *Across the sands of Dee!*

The first song that was ever sung in the house is sung by the first underhousemaid while Griselda and the Eye are still on their honeymoon; her name is long ago forgotten but the song is there. The Eye is a Whig but his housemaid sings 'Bonnets of Blue' for the Tories. She has another song and that is called 'Rosaleen, the Prairie Flower': –

> *On the distant pra – irie*
> *Turn ti tum, tum ti tum, tum tee tee . . .*

There is of course Mrs Crabbe's song: –

> Chick chick chick chick chick chick
> Lay a little egg for me.

There are songs in the drawing-room and kitchen and nursery; there are ballads and laments; so many of the songs are so mournful and so many of them are Scottish: –

> And he bowed doon his bonny head,
> And red, oh red, the blude ran doon.

The children's songs are sad too: dead children; dead kittens; dead birds; but as brisk as Mrs Crabbe is a certain nursery song that all the children like: –

> My mother told me
> I never should
> Play with the gypsies
> In the wood.
> And she told me
> If I did,
> She would rap my fingers
> With the teapot lid.
> 'Your hair won't curl,
> Your shoes won't shine
> And I shall not consider you
> A little girl of mine.'

There are war songs, of five wars: –

Say – a – prayer
For – the – boys – over – there.[1]

'Pshaw!' said Rolls and turned the wireless off.

There are carols. The carols, like the hymns and the nursery rhymes, are an integral part of the house and, in their simplicity, they and the bald matter-of-fact nursery rhymes are the least sentimental of all the songs.

The holly and the ivy now are full well grown,
Of all the trees that spring in wood the holly bears the crown.
The holly bears a blossom as white as lily flower,
And Mary bore sweet Jesus Christ to be our sweet saviour.
The holly bears a berrie as red as any blood
And Mary bore sweet Jesus Christ to do poor sinners good.
The holly bears a prickle as sharp as any thorn
And Mary bore sweet Jesus Christ on Christmas day on the morn.
The holly bears a bark, as bitter as any gall . . .

And

Tar-ra-ra-boom-de-ay . . .

the barrel organ cuts across it from the Place outside where the Italian with his black felt hat and long cold nose and white teeth and brilliant ingratiating smile is standing by the kerb, bowing, while his little monkey with its cheeks well pouched sits on the organ top in its red flannel dress.

1 Copyright 1917 by Leo Feist, Inc.

There are surprisingly few lullabies. Did Griselda then, not sing lullabies? There is the song she sings, that Uncle Billy of the Children's Hour sings in Verity's time, the song about the ship laden with lovely things; but no, on the whole, Griselda does not sing lullabies.

It was nearly dusk now on the landing. The glow from the electric fire fell softly on the carpet and it made a smaller circumference in the increasing darkness. The house, outside the small circle, was in less than twilight; half-light.

'Give them candles to-night,' said the Marchesa. 'Candles everywhere.'

Twilight. Half-light. Candlelight.

'Selina put in gas,' said Rolls. 'I always regretted it.'

'You put in electric light. Why did you Rollo? You never used the house?'

'I didn't want it to miss anything,' said Rolls slowly.

They were silent and, round them, the house, that did not miss the smallest thing, manifested itself in stirrings, rustlings, tickings, the train vibrations, the sound, again, of a mouse.

'*I am the house dog.*'

'*I am the house cat.*'

'*Chick chick chick chick chick chick.*'

'*Take three tenses.*'

'*And last of all, before we say "Good night", to Verity Dane of London ...*'

'*You are beautiful. Beautiful.*'

'*You understand about the soubise?*'

'*John, how do you pronounce Popocatepetl?*'

'*Can't he get boots in Worcestershire?*'

'When you said "All right", you meant all right for flying didn't you?'

With his eyes open Rolls stared at the gathering darkness; at the glow of the fire, at the dusk of the Place outside the window, where the snow flakes showed themselves white for a moment as they fell. He opened the window as Grizel came upstairs. He could not see more than her figure and the oval of her face.

'Look Grizel,' he said as she came up to him.

'What are you doing Uncle Rolls?' Her voice sounded muf-fled.

'Looking for the lamplighter,' said Rolls and then chuckled as he drew back his hand and sleeve. 'But look Grizel. Real snow.'

EVENING

Now it was evening.

In every window of every house the curtains and blinds were drawn more meticulously than any parlourmaid or any Athay or Slater ever draws them; they were drawn to the cracks, sealing them. On the pavement the street lamps were in darkness and a car coming along the Place had its lights hooded, deflected down on the road. Evensong was going on in the church but it had no bell to make it known. No bells, no lights; only a hush and darkness; but there was going to be a moon.

Presently the city, in spite of all mortals could do, presently the city would be lit.

It is evening.

Griselda has just come in. Athay opens the door to her. Griselda is not like Grizel, she has no key for herself. The keys are on the Eye's key ring, or else in Athay's charge. Griselda has only a large heavy bunch of household keys. She loses them frequently. 'Where are my keys?' 'Children, look for my keys.' That is very often said by Griselda. The Eye laughs; everything is carefully locked up and the keys are often lost.

Athay opens the door. 'Miss Dunn is waiting in the drawing-room, madam. And the master said would you please go to him as soon as you came in. Cook would like to speak to you before dinner if you have a moment.'

'One minute Athay. I must go upstairs first. Send Agnes to me.' She goes upstairs drawing off her gloves, loosening the wide satin strings of her bonnet that is made of gold-brown plush with a quilling round the edge of it of that same satin ribbon in lavender and brown. Athay comes upstairs with the parcels that he has taken from the footman. This last year the Eye has kept his carriage, a landau with a pair of bays.

'Did Miss Dunn say what she wanted Athay?'

'No madam. She seemed – a little upset.'

'Ask her if she will mind waiting a few minutes. Is there a fire for her? I must see your master first.'

Mrs Proutie rustles from the service door. 'May I come, m'm? There isn't too much time.'

'Yes Cook?'

'Huskisson 'as no soles for to-night m'm. You particularly said soles so I thought I better 'ad arsk. And did Athay show you the flowers? I told him he 'ad better not do them till you 'ad seen them. The iris are such a funny colour of blue. You ordered them for purple and mauve I told him, not an 'orrible colour like that.'

Lena skips downstairs. She is a well-grown little girl of six with her brown straight hair tied up in bows over each temple, tartan bows to match her wide-skirted tartan dress that has a low neck and short sleeves. Selina's elbows all her life are cold. It is from those early dresses. Now she is bright-eyed, alert. She has been watching for Griselda and is determined to catch her.

'Mother. *Listen!*

A ree, a ree, I wander,
A penny piece I squander—'

'Lena. Go with Nurse.'

'If I were Elizabeth,' remarks Lena, 'you would listen.' And she kicks the chair.

'Miss Lena what a naughty wicked fib!'

'Little girls should be seen and not 'eard,' says Mrs Proutie.

Agnes, Griselda's young maid, comes in and takes her gloves and bonnet. 'About to-night ma'am,' says Agnes, 'will you wear the black? Or the net? There is a little hole in the net that wants a darn. It won't show if I hide it in the folds. But I must get on. It is almost time for you to dress. And that poor Mrs Trelawny is downstairs, crying. She says her husband has been beating her again and sold all the clothes off the little girl's back.'

'A prawn mousse m'm?'

'It *might* be the beginning of a rash it seems to me. I have his throat tied round in flannel.'

'The answer for Lady Lomax madam, and the master is waiting.'

In a wondering voice Griselda inquires from Athay what time the Eye came home. He had come in at half-past five says Athay and gone straight to the study, where Athay had taken him a brandy-and-soda. Come in, gone straight, peaceably, without impediment, and shut himself in the study where, sacrosanct, Athay had served him with a brandy-and-soda. And what shall I have? asks Griselda of herself. I have had no tea. I shall have dinner of course. Yes, presently. But how presently?

'Lena, not just now dear,' says Griselda. 'I shall come up to Freddie by and by Nurse. I had better look at the flowers Athay. I particularly wanted them mauve, and tell Miss Dunn I shall be in directly. About the mousse, Mrs Proutie, now let me think. Give Mrs Trelawny something hot, Agnes, cocoa; I must just write an answer to this note.'

She goes towards the door of her room but they follow her.

'Shall I get out the net then ma'am?'

'Wear the black Mother. Oh Mother, I do so want a blue silk Sunday dress with a ruche here and a ruche here and lace—'

'Shall I take Miss Lena upstairs with me ma'am?'

'If you could spare a minute to decide m'm.'

'Just as you think Cook,' says Griselda. 'Anything.'

'In that case—' says Mrs Proutie indignantly and, her bosom indignantly bouncing, she goes out to the backstair door.

'Could I have the note madam? The man says he has a long ride.'

'The net . . .?'

'Well if I can't have a new dress may I wear my new cherry sash to come down to dessert?'

'And the master says will you come down madam.'

Woman was created from a rib in Adam's side, but by an odd arrangement it turns out in a house that the man is the head, remains aloof, the children are the hands that go out and touch, experiment, contact; and Oh! cries Griselda shutting the door and going to her desk, Oh! I should like to be the hands. But the woman is the heart . . . and if she stopped beating for a minute, thinks Griselda irritably sitting down to write the note, if she stopped beating for a second the whole house would stop! 'Lena dear not now.' 'By and by Nurse.' 'A prawn mousse Cook?' 'I had better look at the flowers.' 'Give Mrs Trelawny a hot drink.' 'Dear Lady Lomax, – Thank you for . . .' 'Tell Mr Dane . . .' 'Please ask Miss Dunn . . .'

Adam's left rib! thinks Griselda, sealing Lady Lomax's note. Soles or prawns. Either or neither. Let the irises be blue or mauve, or purple or crimson or black. Let Mrs Trelawny be beaten purple and blue like the iris. Tell Miss Dunn to go away. Tell Freddie's spots to go away. Never Lena never. Never. Tell your master that your mistress has run away.

On Griselda's desk are the parcels, the things she has bought this afternoon: the Eye's collars, on approval, because no one is allowed to choose the Eye's collars but the Eye; Griselda is not sure, either, she remembered his size. Freddie's medicine; the salt-cellar repaired; cutting-out scissors for Nurse; Griselda has a suspicion that these are the third pair this year but she has not kept count of them. I should have counted, says Griselda. I ought somehow to have contrived to have kept count. Buttons; tape; shirt buttons; the boys' handkerchiefs. The candles for Lena's cake; a little toy, a wooden apple with a tiny tea-set, wooden painted with roses, that I thought Elizabeth – but of course I ought not to have bought it. How funny, thinks Griselda, to have to spend most of your life trying to like the things you can't like, and the rest dissembling how much you like the things you like – you love. Elizabeth's toy, then: the library books.

She stops. She picks up one of them and opens it. *Popocatepetl* – She reads and then she looks more closely: –

Popocatepetl, a mountain whose pleated sides take on the most vivid reflections; sometimes at sunset the peak rises, rose and flame and soft convolvulus blue under its cap of snow.

She stands by the table with her eyes shut. Then gently, with a rustle of her skirts, she turns and goes downstairs, giving Athay the folded note for Lady Lomax as she passes to the study door.

'Where have you been?' says the Eye. 'Why didn't you come down? I wanted you.'

'So did everyone else.'

'Leave them to manage by themselves,' says the Eye. 'They know their work. Let them go on with it.'

'It isn't as simple as that,' says Griselda and she speaks in a faraway voice.

'It is perfectly simple. Look my dear. I come in. I go straight to my study and who interferes with me?'

'Yes who?' says Griselda, and she says, thinking again, 'Woman was created from a rib in Adam's left side wasn't she?'

'Under his heart,' says the Eye.

That is clever, diabolically clever. That disarms her. That is how the Eye loves Griselda and how she is joined to him, by a transcendental mystery of the flesh; and it must be transcendent, thinks Griselda, because they are obviously, in an earthly sense, of very different flesh. There is this bond, this joining, and it has become intrinsic; torn or broken it would bleed almost mortally. If she were free, to go free, suddenly set free, would she go? Griselda cannot answer that question. Presently – Presently – that word is her shield. 'Presently,' says Griselda. 'Not now. Not now Lena. By and by Nurse – Tell Miss Dunn I shall be in directly. Presently there shall after all be a prawn mousse – and the irises shall be mauve – and Mrs Trelawny, after cocoa, shall be given consolation – presently, I shall come.'

'John,' says Griselda aloud. 'How do you pronounce Popocatepetl?'

The post came. The big double knock sounded through the

house and Proutie came upstairs and went along the hall to collect the letters. He walked in the track of many thousand other evenings, when the knock sounds over and over again, the same knock; knock upon knock. Athay goes to get the evening post; Slater goes; the letters are taken into the study or drawing-room on a salver; those for the rest of the household spread out on the chest in the hall by the blue-and-white bowl.

Proutie took two letters and a postcard out of the cage. The postcard was a printed one: –

MESSRS. WARRINGTON AND RESEDALE
Beg to announce their
SPECIAL PRE-CHRISTMAS WHITE SALE.

There was an air-mail letter for Grizel from New York with gay blue and red edges. There was one letter for Rolls: –

General Sir Roland Ironmonger Dane, K.C.B., D.S.O.

On the flap of the envelope was printed a firm's name: –

WILLOUGHBY, PAXTON, LOW AND WILLOUGHBY

Proutie took it up to Rolls in his dressing-room, where Rolls was sitting.

'The post Mr Rolls.'

'Go away,' said Rolls. 'Leave me alone.'

Proutie put the letter on the table at Rolls's elbow and went away.

Years before there is another letter, a letter written by Rolls in answer to many letters of Selina's.

She reads it in her room sitting in the blue-and-white armchair on which this afternoon, dressing to have tea with Pax, after she had been asleep, Grizel tossed down her pyjamas and left, standing by it on the rug, a pair of swansdown slippers that she called her 'scuffs'.

Selina as a girl has a swansdown muff, dyed violet with a rose in it, but she keeps it tidily in tissue paper in the cupboard; she does not throw her things about nor leave them on the floor. As she reads Rolls's letter, Selina is not a girl; she is an elderly woman and that day she feels old. *You ask me, Lena, why I don't come home. That is a question that is rather difficult to answer. I seem to have a distaste for the house.*

And for me, thinks Selina staring stiffly over the muslin blind. *A distaste.* There is nothing dramatic in the word that Rolls has chosen but it is deadening to Selina. *That is the truth. Whether it is the whole truth I can't tell. I should like to see you. Can you lunch with me? I shall be sailing sometime next month.*

Lunch with me! My Rollo! says Selina and her hand holding the letter is stiff and cold.

'Why does Rollo write so seldom?' That, long ago, is Pelham's voice.

'He is working very hard.'

'He doesn't regret going out there?'

'Why should he regret it?' Selina's voice is high. 'No certainly he doesn't. It was a wonderful chance for him.'

'Has he been crossed in love?' asks Pelham idly.

Why should Pelham ask that?

'He is so changed,' said Pelham. 'His letters are so changed.'

'Nonsense. He is working hard as I told you. He is a Dane. All the Danes are ambitious.'

'Rollo was different,' says Pelham slowly. 'I thought he was different,' he corrects himself. '*Has* he been crossed in love?'

'Why should you ask me?' cries Selina passionately and defensively.

'Good heavens Selina! I thought you might know, that is all.'

Now Selina goes to the window. She looks down on the garden, on its long walls; its black earth beds; its paths; the syringa bushes; the row of lime-trees; it is autumn and the leaves have been raked into a pile and presently, to-morrow or the next day, there will be a bonfire and the smoke, leaf-smelling, country-smelling, will blow out towards the road. In the bed are a few Michaelmas daisies. Selina has seen it so every year for fifty-eight years; she has seen the garden more than twenty thousand times but she never remembers seeing it as quiet and empty as it is now. Where, she wonders suddenly, are the Jewish children from next door? When the plane-tree boughs were still green, she remembers, they used to build their *sukkoth* on the balcony for their feast. She can remember looking down, not from this window but from the one above, to see it. I used to be scolded for the smuts on my cheek, thinks Selina. There is no one to scold her now. Suddenly she seems to see the little comic figure in a dowdy bonnet of Miss Dunn.

'What is there to show for it,' says Miss Dunn, 'when you are old and perhaps left alone? You haven't been anywhere, done anything, and there is no time left—' And it was Miss Dunn who said of Griselda, 'She was rewarded. She was loved.'

'Is it so important to be loved?' asked Lark.

Lark! It was all because of Lark, thinks Selina, as she has

thought so often. Lark went and Pelham went and Rollo never came back. What weapon had Selina against Lark? And yet Lark had no weapons, she was defenceless. Lark had nothing at all. If I had been different would it have been different? asks Selina and immediately she covers up that thought in her mind and pushes away the sight of Miss Dunn.

I am like a quince, thinks Selina and she is deliberately, slightly proud of that. I am like a quince. Some women are like those sweet oranges, bergamots, that you stick full of cloves, each an experience with a spice, and as the bergamots wither they make an incense, a perfume. I don't. I have none of these spices. I am sour.

Still she thinks of Lark. Lark, she remembers, is now only thirty-six. Lark has been in London that summer. *Among the visitors the beautiful young Marchesa Zacca del Laudi in a toque of parma violets . . . ; I saw the attractive Marchesa Zacca del Laudi . . . ; . . . wearing the del Laudi emeralds . . . ; . . . the Marchesa Zacca del Laudi in grey lace was in the Royal box . . . ; The Marchese and his beautiful English wife . . .* 'Have you news of Miss Lark?' It is Proutie who asks that. 'None whatever Proutie. None,' Selina answers. 'You have always hated me,' says Lark.

I have always hated you, Selina agrees. I always wanted you out of the house. I thought you were gone, that I had dismissed you, from my thoughts and from the house . . . but after Lark has gone her presence grows stronger. Pelham felt your power that last summer, and Rollo, says Selina.

Rollo, all that summer, before he goes to Afghanistan with Fitzgerald, makes excuses to come home on leave. In all its excitement, with this possibility opening before him – with his transfer to the Piffers with the consultations with Uncle

Bunny – with the polo and the Pumas for whom he played – through it all Rollo is beset by a vision. It is mingled for him of sunlight and summer and flowers, though afterwards he says he has no time for flowers; in it the light is a clear sunny light but with it the summer is a vision of green. He can smell the flowers and they are intrinsic; they are always there. Was Lark singing in the garden? No, he knows that she was not. At Wiltshire Place the gardens are not green; this is a garden green with groves, and as soon as he says that, he sees it clearly; there are groves of trees; there is a stream and there are swans. The strange thing is, that though this comes through Lark's singing, in the garden she is silent; she is not singing, nor talking, nor laughing, but looking at him and he sees her, her hair, her trailing skirts, and the ribbon in her hat. In this vision she is Rollo's; she belongs to him; but as soon as he arrives at Wiltshire Place he does not pursue her but avoids her. 'It is fatal to marry young, unless you have money.' They all tell him that. 'He ruined his career, silly chap,' they say. 'You are a youngest son, you have your own way to make,' says Pelham. 'Rollo? But of course Rollo can't think of marriage for ages,' says Selina. Lark says nothing at all.

'I could never remember you,' said Rolls to the Marchesa. 'The more I thought about you, later, the more I wanted to remember, the less I could.'

'Perhaps you didn't look at me sufficiently,' suggested the Marchesa. 'You were rather busy that summer looking at yourself.'

'No. I was afraid to look at you,' said Rolls.

Nothing ever really happened between them, argues Selina, looking at the daisies that grow a sooty bitter purple in the old earth of the beds. Nothing happened. It only might have been. It was slight. It was impermanent. Lark ran away; Rollo went out to Afghanistan with Fitzgerald; Lark married the Marchese; it was made impermanent. It remained.

'Won't you come and see me Rollo? Come to the house again? Come home?'

I am staying at my club not half a mile away. I am in India, China, Basutoland, ten thousand miles across the ocean. What difference is there? 'No Selina. I shall not come home. No Selina, no.'

It is an evening in November, eighteen ninety, and Rollo has been to a levee.

He comes in afterwards to surprise the family but the family is out. Slater, eyeing his magnificence, says they will not be long. 'There is a dinner to-night,' says Slater and he adds, 'It is Miss Lark's birthday, Mr Rollo.'

'Lark's birthday?' asks Rollo and for a moment he is silent. Then he asks, 'How old is she Slater?'

Slater smiles; between his tufts of white hair left either side of a bald pate, Slater's pale face looks all at once human. 'She is eighteen, Mr Rollo. A lovely young lady if I may say so. She came out this spring. She has been very much admired.'

'Has she?' says Rollo, and more thoughtfully, '*Has* she?' This is disconcerting. If one has a vision one rather expects it to remain one's own, not to develop independence, or worse, to be in danger of becoming someone else's vision. For the first time it occurs to Rollo that he will have – or have not – to make some definite move over Lark. He cannot go on dreaming of her and avoiding her forever. But I am not ready yet, he complains. It seems however that Lark is ready. Rollo is put out. I liked her best as a dream, he might have complained. That is how she suited me best. But Lark will not be a dream; she is flesh and blood, with admirers; a vision in fact, capable of giving, not a slap in the face, or yes even a slap in the face because she may not care for Rollo, but certainly a stab in the back. Admirers. That of course rouses Rollo and pricks him. But just now? he asks doubtfully, Now? When everything is on the verge of fruition? Fruition because the seeds were laid long long ago, and the plant has been so carefully watched and grown. Now? It really is very inconvenient of Lark to have grown up just now.

Rollo understands precisely why his presence has been required at this levee. He knows that there is a possibility that is more than a possibility that when he goes to India it may not be to join his new regiment, or even to stay in India at all. His transfer is according to plan. 'Fitzgerald asked at once if you were in the Indian Army,' said Uncle Bunny, with a chuckle. 'I was able to assure him that you were. Quick work, my boy.' There is to be a mission to Afghanistan. Lord Fitzgerald, the Fitzgerald who was with General Roberts at Dakka and Char-asiab, and Kandahar in 'seventy-nine and 'eighty, Lord Fitzgerald is going out to take over the Afghan Army and remodel it for the Amir on British lines. Lord Fitzgerald? Yes, Uncle Bunny knows him well but there is no backstair way with old Fitzgerald. It is his policy to choose his personal staff himself and only on Rollo himself can the choice depend. Rollo is introduced one afternoon at Ranelagh. 'Piffers?' said Fitzgerald with an approving glance. It was his policy also to choose for this only officers of the Indian Army. This afternoon at the far end of the room, Rollo has seen Fitzgerald looking at him; he sees Fitzgerald nod and say something to the exalted personage beside him; he sees the exalted personage look across too and answer. Later they pass Rollo and Fitzgerald stops. 'Well young Dane, the game didn't go your way after all. Hard luck. You played damned well. Well, see you soon.' No, says Rollo slowly thinking of Lark. No it wouldn't be possible or wise. I couldn't possibly. Not now. As soon as he says it, he is filled with a burning desire to see her and to know who those admirers are.

'I suppose she goes to dances Slater?'

'Oh yes, Mr Rollo. They are going on to a dance to-night. The first of the winter dances as you might say. In Orme Square. Mrs Kingdon Charles.'

'Mrs Charles? We had children's parties there.' And he says, 'Will you have a note sent round for me Slater? I should like to go too. Who is dining here?'

'Dinner is for ten. There are Mr and Mrs and Miss Cresswell. Sir Arthur and Lady Bartram. Major Allison and an Italian gentleman, Mr Rollo, the Marchese Zacca del Laudi.'

'Zacca del Laudi?' says Rollo in surprise and whistles.

'He very often comes these days,' says Slater with pride and with meaning.

'The devil he does,' says Rollo. 'Wait Slater. I shall give you that note.'

When he has written it he draws circles and faces on the blotting paper. Rollo can see, with the dazzling clarity which all the Danes possess when assessing money or position, the exact difference between himself and the Marchese; that the Marchese is a funny little man, almost mannikin, does not occur to him; if it did it would hardly seem to affect the position. But how did she meet him? thinks Rollo. Pelham, or Selina, must have been wangling some good invitations. To him there does not appear to be anything reprehensible in this; wangling, and using friends, or making friends to use them, is merely sensible to Rollo. Was not his own godfather, Uncle Bunny, chosen to be of use to him and is he not being of extreme use? No really, just now, I mustn't think of it. It isn't possible, decides Rollo. Anyway she probably wouldn't look at me with the Marchese and probably that is just as well, but as he says that he is filled, simply and completely, with a biting jealousy.

He tries to remember Lark exactly and he finds he cannot. 'I never could remember you,' said Rolls to the Marchesa. 'The more I thought of you, the more I wanted to remember, the less I could.'

As a matter of fact, no one afterwards can remember Lark that summer. The reason is that she is never the same; never fixed; never comprehensive. There is no idea or mood that lasts for more than a day. Meanwhile she behaves with a gaiety that is attractive and that has a spice of wantonness in it. 'That little Ingoldsby girl is a flirt,' say the mothers disapprovingly and they could shake Edith or Mary or Dorothy sitting there, bare shoulders and wreath of forget-me-nots, quite dumb while that little nobody walks away with anyone she chooses on the floor. Of course, Lark really should not be at these dances 'but that Pelham—' 'Pelham,' says Selina bitterly, 'Pelham is bewitched.'

Perhaps he is. Afterwards, he finds he cannot remember Lark then either. Was she serious or gay? He knows that she was gay but the remembrance is oddly one of seriousness. Nor can he remember her face; her dresses, yes; her voice; her hand with his birthday bracelet on its wrist; but he cannot remember her face. She kisses Pelham good night and he horribly resents that sleepy trusting childish kiss, but he can never bring himself to stop it;

he remembers all day the scent of her skin, the brushing of her hair against his, and the light unnoticing touch of her lips; it makes him angry in a way in which he has never felt angry before. Pelham is a mild little man but he could sometimes hurt Lark physically for the way in which she kisses him good night.

Lark wears a pale-green dress; a white one; white taffeta with a chenille fringe; she has a cream tulle dress with ribbons of petunia and black. She has fans – she leaves one on the hall table; it is white, of ostrich feathers, with an ivory handle. How does Lark come to have such a beautiful fan? Pelham gives it to her. Pelham is bewitched. 'You are ridiculously extravagant over Lark,' says Selina. 'You never gave such things to me or Rollo.' Flowers come for Lark on ball nights. 'Will you be at Ponsonby House on Tuesday?' 'Are you going to the Neves'?' Flowers arrive in long white cardboard boxes with a card, and always, lately, there is a card with a small gold coat of arms. Proutie takes them up to her. 'Solomon's lilies,' says Proutie gravely as he hands them to her at her door. Proutie is fond of Lark but if he too were asked exactly what she looked like then, he too would not be able to say.

Now, as Slater takes Rollo's note, Lark herself, with Pelham, comes into the drawing-room. She stops still just inside the door looking at Rollo and Rollo at the writing table looks back at her, and slowly, still looking, he stands up. Neither of them notices Pelham as he comes past Lark into the room.

'Good Lord!' says Pelham as he sees Rollo. 'Good Lord!'

Rollo does not notice him. He looks at Lark. She is wearing a long dark-green coat and the ermine cap and stole and muff that arrived for her that morning.

'Ermine,' says Selina reverently as she turns back the tissue paper. '*Ermine!*' She picks up the card that has again the small gold coat of arms: *Con omaggio. Vostro devotissimo*, GUIDO. 'The Marchese! But you can't accept this from him Lark.'

'Why not?' asks Lark.

'No lady could.'

'I am not a lady,' says Lark serenely. 'You must remember how ill-bred I am, Selina. You are always reminding me of that. And if someone nice – and he is nice, poor little man,' says Lark with her eyes gentle – 'If it makes him happy to give me things why shouldn't I accept them?'

'But you should take him seriously. He is serious,' says Selina.

'I know he is, and I am sorry,' says Lark and then she laughs. 'But I could put him in my pocket.'

Now the fur looks brilliant against Lark's skin and hair and happy eyes; she does not attempt to hide the happiness. It is there as she sees Rollo.

'Is this new?' asks Pelham walking round Rollo. 'I have never seen it before.' Rollo is in full dress: high black boots, white breeches, dark-green tunic frogged with black, and a crimson sash. He looks immensely tall, a huge young man. Dear Pelham! thinks Lark as she watches Pelham walking round him, Don't do that. You look like a bantam round a fighting cock. Rollo looks at her over Pelham's head and she sees such wonder and recognition on his face that she is lifted up on wings of tumultuous joy. Steady, says Lark to herself, Be calm. 'Hullo Rollo,' she says aloud as she comes to join them in the room. He does not answer. He is perfectly still. Then: 'I have been to a levee,' he says suddenly transferring his attention to Pelham.

'A levee? Well really Rollo my boy, that new dress is magnificent. Look at the sash Lark. Did you ever see a better colour?'

Lark picks up one of the heavy white gloves and slips her hand into it. It is still warm and hastily she takes her hand out and drops the glove back on the chair.

'You seem about seven feet high,' says Pelham and there is a wistful look in his eyes. 'Magnificent. Really most impressive.'

He becomes aware that he is talking into a silence. Lark and Rollo in the same instant hear that too.

'Was the Queen there?' asks Lark. 'It is much colder—' begins Rollo.

He breaks off and Lark asks again, 'Was the Queen there?'

'No, only the Prince of Wales. The Queen is at Osborne.'

'Yes of course. The Queen would be at Osborne.'

After a moment Lark says again, 'Of course. The Queen would be at Osborne wouldn't she?'

Pelham looks from one of them to the other. 'Lark, it is time you were getting dressed,' he says slowly.

'Why wasn't I told about this birthday?' asks Rollo.

'We didn't think you would be interested.'

'You were wrong,' says Rollo, his eyes on Lark. 'I have just written to Mrs Charles to ask if I can join you to-night.'

'O – h!' That escapes from Lark's lips and there is no mistaking it. It is a sigh of bliss.

Pelham objects. He has to object or stifle. He makes the only objection he can think of: 'Is that very polite to Mrs Charles? At the last moment?'

'Oh Pelham *dear*!' says Lark. 'Don't be so stuffy.'

Stuffy. The word rings on the air and Pelham reddens to the tips of his ears. 'Well at any rate,' he says, 'it is time for you to dress.'

'I shall have to come as I am,' says Rollo.

'That won't matter,' says Pelham, who is always fair. 'There will be plenty of full dress there. Lark dear.' He is at the door.

'You go,' says Lark.

Neither she nor Rollo notices when he goes.

'Did Pelham give you a birthday present?'

'This.' She shows her bracelet, a little chain locked with a heart of sapphires and small rose diamonds.

'Oh ho!' says Rollo. 'How poetical! Quite expensive too – for Pelham. He was done though. The stones are poor.'

'How can you be so horrid!'

'He is no judge of a stone, old Pelham,' says Rollo, and he looks at Lark. 'And the Marchese? What did he send?'

Lark slowly blushes. Suddenly and sharply, she regrets the ermine. She recognizes that this large young man, whom she has idealized into a cardboard hero, possesses a very real power to make her behave. If I were with you, thinks Lark, I could behave. I would be good and sensible. She thinks back over her behaviour that summer and her blush grows deeper.

'Look at me Lark?'

As she looks, she sees that he is freckled lightly along his cheekbones and down his nose, and that seems to make him more real too. She is delighted, lifted again on those wings.

'So you will live in Italy, and spend your time eating macaroni and going to the Opera.'

'I shall if I want to,' says Lark joyfully.

'I shouldn't Lark,' says Rollo coming close to her. 'They eat Larks in Italy.'

'I – must go and get dressed,' says Lark.

'What are you going to wear? Wear white,' says Rollo.

'It is white; white tulle with knots of black velvet and

white marguerites with black centres. It is French. So lovely Rollo.'

'Did Pelham give you that too?'

'Poor Pelham has to give me everything.'

That should come as a warning to Rollo, though he has a surge of desire to oust Pelham, never to let Pelham give her anything again. I forbid you to accept a thing, anything from Pelham, but at the same time he feels a brake. You can't live on your pay, it says. Don't be mad. Don't be so foolish. He is checked and he prepares to fortify himself, and then finds he has said, 'Well I am going to give you a birthday present too, do you hear? And it will make Pelham open his eyes.'

Lark works on extravagance like yeast on dough but now she says, 'No Rollo. Don't. Don't please. Please don't. I don't want anything at all.'

'Want it or not,' says Rollo. 'You are going to have it, because I want to give it to you, see? And no one is going to give you a better one. Not even your Marchese.'

Oh! thinks Lark with a pang. Ermine! And Selina will tell him. I know she will. She shuts her eyes because she is too happy to keep them open any longer. Keep calm, says Lark. Help me to keep calm, she prays. Help me to keep my face, and my head. This comes to everyone. I must remember that. It is a common experience. It comes to everyone. Everyone falls in love. But I haven't fallen in love, she objects. I am merely confirmed in it. But it feels anything but mere; it feels heady and giddy. Keep your head, says Lark sharply. It is the commonest thing on earth. And it doesn't always make you happy. There is no reason why it should. Don't go leaping to conclusions, says Lark severely and she opens her eyes and smiles dazzlingly at Rollo.

Rollo has been saying 'Fitzgerald' sternly to himself. Fitzgerald. Fitzgerald. Fitzgerald. He forgets it completely as Lark smiles and in a curious voice which is quite unlike Rollo's, husky and blurred, he says 'Lark?'

'I – must go and get dressed,' says Lark.

The house has its occasions.

There are the occasions that come regularly in season; they give meaning and rhythm to the year. The earliest of all, and the one that flutters out of fashion first, is St Valentine's Day; who knows now that that is the day on which the birds are supposed officially to mate? Selina is the last person in the house to get a Valentine; it is a pretty one, of paper lace, painted with lover's knots and cherubs, but Selina whole-heartedly laughs at it and puts it in the waste paper basket. It is anonymous. Next in the year is April Fool's Day, but this is not, in the Dane household, for grown-ups but strictly for children and servants, just as Derby Day is not for children, but for grown-ups and servants; Slater once wins a hundred pounds. Then comes Easter, and Easter includes Lent: no marmalade for breakfast, no jam for tea, fish twice a week, no sweets; and Palm Sunday, when at Children's Service small crosses of palm are given out; and Good Friday, with hot cross buns for break-fast, and church on a week-day; until finally, with a burst of happiness, it is Easter Sunday. It is Griselda's custom, and later Selina's, to send flowers to her friends at Easter. Pelham, Selina, Roly, later Lark, all help to deliver them on the after-noon of Saturday: lilacs, jonquils, hyacinths in pots; the first daffodils. The colours of Easter are white and yellow; the church is decorated in yellow and white: the children are wearing, perhaps, their new white spring coats and bonnets;

but the eggs at breakfast are painted in every colour: scarlet, pink, and yellow and blue.

The Dane family know nothing about Midsummer's Day but they are aware, from the family next door, of the Jewish feasts; in return for the branches, at the Passover a present of unleavened bread is sent in. Rolls when he first saw Ry-Vita was irresistibly reminded of that bread. Then there is August Bank Holiday: once Pelham takes Roly to see Greenwich Fair to the annoyance of Selina. A few days later, every year, comes the beginning of the summer holiday. Other people go away in August but the Eye takes September for better fishing. Every year it is the same, to Locheven in Argyll; the furnished house, St Mynns, that the Eye takes every year. There are trunks and valises in the hall; there are baskets: lunch and tea baskets, travelling baskets, Nurse's Japan basket, the Eye's fishing basket; there are his rods and landing net; there are camp stools and strapped umbrellas and plaid rugs. The carriage is at the door for the Eye, and Griselda with, perhaps, Selina and one of the boys; the cabs stand behind it and Athay is sent ahead to take up the bookings, and to arrange the compartments, three, reserved by the Eye to Stirling. Some families, as Lena says longingly, have their own trains.

Then with the autumn come bonfires –

> *Remember, remember,*
> *The Fifth of November.*

'Street-boy games,' Selina tells Roly scornfully, but Roly and old Athay let off fireworks in the garden. On this day, on the whole five days from the first of the month, a license to pester is given to all boys; guys are dragged in soap on wheels: 'Penny for the Guy. Penny for the Guy' – and there is the sound of bangs and sizzlings from the fireworks, rockets and crackers and Catherine wheels let off in back gardens, and a crude exciting smell of gunpowder.

On every anniversary of their wedding day, the Eye gives Griselda violets and a piece of jewellery. She kisses him thoughtfully.

'What are you thinking of Griselda?'

'Dear, did you remember to tell Athay about the wine?'

There is always a dinner in the evening but the Eye knows it is not that of which she is thinking.

'You like the earrings Griselda?'

'Yes dear, very very much.'

The Eye sighs.

There have been birthdays of course all through the year. On Selina's, which comes in December, the Danes give their annual children's party. From half-past three, carriages and cabs drive up and children in coats and shawls are set down with their governesses and nurses, carrying their party slippers in bags. The coats and shawls are left in Griselda's room; the dining-room has added little tables to its large one, and there are jellies in glasses and cream puffs and mince pies and Roly's favourite pink meringues with raspberry jam. The birthday cake gives out a smell of hot wax from the candles and damp icing. The drawing-room is cleared for dancing and games and there is a conjuror on the landing. 'Is there a rabbit in this hat? There is. I put it there myself. No deception. Now – *Abracadabracadabra*. No? No! Odd! It is a Union Jack.'

Then comes Christmas. It begins by Mrs Proutie's making the puddings and by the puddings' being stirred. During the weeks after that the Eye, and later Pelham, brings back from the office wooden drums of fruit, raisins and dried figs, and Carlsbad Plums in long boxes, and once some Chinese dried lichees; Chinese too are the jars of ginger. They may bring a case or two of wine and tea, and a special blend of coffee; these are mostly mysterious business presents. Then comes the holly and the mistletoe, and wreaths are made and mantelpieces decorated; a piece of mistletoe is hung in the kitchen passage and there are scufflings and squeaks when anyone comes to the back door.

From the grocer's come oranges in silver paper, and chestnuts and other nuts and all-spice, and from the poulterer's the turkey arrives and is exhibited, naked and enormous, a few black spines of feathers sticking out from it, its neck hanging down and a bluish tinge showing in its flesh colour where the skin is stretched over its bones. 'I won't eat it,' says Roly but he forgets when the Christmas tree is bought and an old German lady in the Square, Gräfin von Schey, sends, as she sends every year, *Leb-kuchen*, honey cakes, baked in old moulds in the shapes of scenes from the life of the Holy Family; she also sends fat china angels to hang on the tree.

The toys are very largely German too; bricks in flaky wooden boxes: pillars and squares and oblongs and half-circles, and there are always magenta half-corners and emerald-green half-cubes; there are wax dolls; trumpets with red tassels; a drum with white lacings; diabolo; a shuttlecock and bat. Cards come with every post; some have real frosting and robins; others are a delicate egg-shell blue with hawthorn and dog-roses in hand painting. There are carol singers, and the bells ringing; and stockings; and morning service; and a quiet private afternoon; and the tree lit in the evening before a Christmas dinner.

On Boxing Day the servants, the tradesmen, the postman, the policeman, the dustman and the crossing sweeper get their Christmas boxes. The Eye brings home a roll of new half-crowns for this.

The Wednesday after Christmas is kept for the pantomime from the time Pelham is five years old. Soon the Eye finds it necessary to take a box, and the box is increasingly filled and then gradually emptied. It dwindles to the Eye, Selina and Roly; and then once to the Eye and Lark. He never takes her again and she lives on the memory until, ten years afterwards, Pelham takes her. 'Would you like to come Lark? We always used to go,' asks Pelham wistfully. 'It is Cinderella.' 'Cinderella!' says Lark. 'I should adore it.' 'Will you come Selina?' 'No thank you,' says Selina, 'I outgrew pantomime before I was sixteen.'

And then, very loudly, tumultuously, at midnight, the bells ring in another New Year's Day and another year begins.

There are other occasions in the house, not seasonal – unforeseen; and they are capable of disrupting the house and altering, if only temporarily, its appearance and its tone. There is the bustle and stir of a birth – the suspense of it, and sometimes that is prolonged. The Eye waits downstairs but often comes up to the landing; Dr Flower's carriage with its greys waits in the Place; Mrs Proutie who is sympathetic becomes upset and clashes the pots and pans. It may be daylight, or night when the carriage lamps are lit; once it was dawn and the sleepy coachman had just extinguished the lamps, when, from the door of the convent, two nuns slipped out on their way to the food markets where they begged for their orphans; they saw the Doctor's carriage and the lighted windows at Number 99 and looked at each other and nodded. 'That will be Mrs Dane.' And they each, under their breath, said a prayer for Griselda and on that moment Elizabeth is born.

As there is birth, so there is death. In their turn, Freddie, Elizabeth, Griselda, the Eye and Juno die in the house. The light is diluted with the dimness of drawn blinds and the air smells differently; sallow little avid-eyed women come from the dress-maker's to measure the mourning, and sallow artificially solemn young men come from the undertaker's to measure the body: the length of the Eye, the little Elizabeth, for the coffin. Wreaths and crosses and flowers are delivered with a subdued knock at the front door, and another young man calls with samples of black-edged note-paper. Death so soon becomes cluttered with life; but in the house, each time, there is true grief, as unalloyed with the years as it is in the first moment of its experience. Griselda rages over Elizabeth with fits of dreadful weeping; the Eye shuts himself into the study and will not open it; Rollo, when the Eye dies, is filled with sorrow and remorse because he remembers the barrier between them and thinks that he had made it; Selina, who has experienced these deaths, finds out that she was only on the fringe of understanding when Juno dies: Juno the pug dog, aged seventeen, adipose, with a pitiful film over her eyes, but with the plush of her coat as glossy and her wallflower markings as brilliant as when Selina first saw her. Juno dies peacefully, comfortably, with a long wheeze and a sigh that, in the quiet room, is curiously like a sudden whirring of wings, as if Juno truthfully had a soul and the soul is taking flight. After she is dead Selina cannot bear the house; she shuts it up and goes to Scarborough and soon after dies herself.

There are other occasions: some large, some small, some serious, some light. The day when the Eye wins seven thousand pounds in a sweepstake; the day when he loses seven thousand pounds in the Glasgow Bank smash; the day Lark comes; the day the boiler explodes in the kitchen maid's face and nearly kills her; Mafeking Day. There are christenings and confirmations; white cakes, white veils; silver mugs, and silver rattles; gold crosses on gold chains and new prayer-books. There is no wedding day; among all the occasions found in the house, there is no wedding day.

On one occasion Selina gives a Christmas party.

Before dinner she brings her guests up on the landing and there by the window is a little Christmas tree decorated, lit with candles, hung with tinsel and witch balls and gifts. Selina has brought these decorations down from the attic; there is the glass bugle that Roly loved; the little glass bells, coloured ice-blue and magenta and holly-red; there is even one of the Gräfin's angels.

'Hullo! Hullo! Hul-lo!' says Mr Baldrick.

'Oh!' says Miss Toft softly and she clasps her hands and her pince-nez glitters. 'Oh! Let me see too! Oh, we are having a lovely party!'

'A happy thought,' says Father Douglas, 'so like you dear Miss Dane' – and he demands loudly: 'Now isn't this a happy thought?'

Selina has suddenly a feeling of sharp regret. I was sentimental, she cries silently. Oh I wish I hadn't been. She watches Mr Baldrick tinkle a little magenta bell.

'Hullo! Oh, I say! Ha ha!' says Mr Baldrick.

Lady Mott is examining the tree through her lorgnettes, horn-rimmed lorgnettes on a wide black ribbon; they are very pronounced but not more noticeable than Lady Mott herself. The lorgnettes examine the tree. 'Sweet,' says Lady Mott acidly.

The Professor has wiped his cheeks with his handkerchief quite openly. 'Not since I left Chermany—' says the Professor.

'I am *so* excited,' says Miss Toft. 'Which do you suppose is for me?'

Selina begins to cut down the parcels with a pair of scissors. 'A little gift for each of you before we go down to have our drinks,' she says, forcing the words to be gay.

'Cocktails?' asks Miss Toft. 'In those sweet little glasses with the red and black cocks? Oh what a lovely party we are having!'

'Ha!' says Mr Baldrick. 'Oh I say, you are spoiling us you know.'

'I never touch them,' says Lady Mott. 'My sciatica—'

'Yes? No?' says the Professor. 'Yes. Now I haf discofered that nuts and orange peel—'

Selina's hands are very shaky to-night she notices, and if she lifts her arm to cut the higher parcels off the tree she has, and knows she will have, like Mrs Sampson, a twinge of pain. Proutie knows that too, forestalls her, and cuts them down for her. Selina feels a surprising response of warmth and gratitude. Dear familiar Proutie, is Selina's thought, and she realizes that she is feeling desolate and more alone amongst her guests than if she were there solitary. I wish I were solitary with the tree. The tree is shining there, its boughs held out holding the bells, the tinsel and the balls and the tiers of lighted candles. It is so pretty. I made it look so pretty, says Selina and yet there is something curiously flat about this bestowing of presents from the tree on these grown-up guests, and the more enthusiastically they respond the more flat it becomes. Selina prefers Lady Mott and the Professor to Miss Toft.

Father Douglas offers Lady Mott a cracker.

'What is it?' asks Lady Mott through her lorgnettes.

'A cracker.'

'No thank you.'

Miss Toft and Mr Baldrick are pulling another. 'It is mine. I have it,' cries Miss Toft.

'No! No! I say! That is damned unfair. What? Ha! Ha!'

'Never mind,' says Miss Toft. 'I shall crown you.' And she puts a tall red crown on Mr Baldrick's head.

'Look here. Someone else must too. It isn't fair. You must all wear caps,' says Mr Baldrick. 'You must all do it you know. Mustn't they?'

The Professor puts a lemon-yellow peaked cap on his dignified head; Father Douglas has a pale pink one; Miss Toft a blue sunbonnet; even Lady Mott, after scrutinizing it, puts on a little white one shaped like a jam tart.

Selina hands the presents round. Miss Toft kisses her and the kiss is dry and very quick. 'A nightdress case! How original!' cries Miss Toft. Lady Mott has a set of bridge cards.

'Ha! Now I can show you a trick. One. Two. Three. Hey presto!' But the trick fails.

'They are my cards,' says Lady Mott.

'One. Two. Three. Hey presto!'

'Oh! How clever! Clever! Oh what a lovely lovely party.'

Selina by the tree is watching her guests. Father Douglas gives a neigh of laughter. '. . . my cards!' says Lady Mott. Mr Baldrick's cap has slipped to one side showing the bald red spot on his head; Miss Toft's face is turned up; under the blue bonnet it is withered into a little hard nut. '. . . absorbs the spittle and acts upon the lining of the stomach,' the Professor is saying gravely under his yellow hat. Selina bends down and picks up her little dog Juno.

Juno attracts attention.

'Oh look!' cries Miss Toft. 'Oh look Juno. Here is a bowl with a bone in it for you.' It is a bowl tied with a red ribbon. It seemed to Selina when she put it there, a simple joke; but now it is not a joke at all and she wants to cry, 'Don't touch it. Leave us alone.' But Miss Toft has it in her hand. 'You must beg for it, you sweetheart little doggie. You lucky girl.'

'Something for the *dog*?' asks Lady Mott.

'Juno doesn't beg,' says Selina shortly taking the bowl from Miss Toft and putting it away behind the tree.

There the Professor is examining the branches with the same thoroughness and gravity he would give to any examination. 'But – this is not goot. There is nothing for Mees Dane.'

'Nothing for Miss Dane.'

'Nothing? For Miss Dane?'

'Oh I say!'

'Nothing for you? Oh Selina *dear*!'

There is an awkward pause. Selina presses Juno closer, closely, to her side. 'Let us go down and have our drinks,' she says and they all begin to talk together as they move towards the stairs. Presently there is the usual cheerful noise and no one need listen or pause or think.

Now like a tide through the house come the children, down from the nursery to the drawing-room. Verity turns the wireless on; he belongs to the International Young Listeners' Friendship League and he has a very special reason for listening in to-day. He is punctual. As he switches it on: '... 'd evening boys and girls,' says the very voice he is expecting. '*This is Aunt Mona and Uncle Billy in the Children's Hour.*'

Griselda, her skirts wide over the carpet as she sits in her chair, is reading to Freddie and Elizabeth. Selina, eight years old now, with her hair held back from her face by a tortoise-shell comb showing her high, intelligent, alert forehead, is leaning over the back of the chair; she is too old to be interested in the story but she stays near Griselda wilfully, partly because she has been asked not to, and partly because she cannot bear to go away. Freddie sits on a stool and Elizabeth is on Griselda's knee, her bright head resting on Griselda's shoulder and her eyes fixed on Griselda's throat where, she has discovered, a little lump works up and down as Griselda speaks.

In the study the Eye is dutifully reading to Roly; he makes a point, punctiliously, of being in from office in time every night to do this; he is punctilious to Roly because he cannot bear the sight of him and this is not because he does not love him but because it was Roly who robbed him of Griselda. No it wasn't Roly, says the Eye. It was myself. It isn't fair to blame Roly. It was my fault, only mine. And he hears his own voice again speaking words that now he will never forget. 'Nine is my lucky number,' says the Eye.

The child Lark is on the landing; she is kneeling by the banisters, looking down into the hall. Presently she will see Slater going to the front door for the evening post, or perhaps Selina will come in, alone or with friends, but certainly in some rustling handsome dress, with earrings and a little hat with flowers or with feathers and a veil, and a short fur jacket or a long coat trimmed with fur, and her voice, high-pitched and certain, filling all the hall. It fascinates Lark to kneel there and look down into the hall. Pelham comes in and gives his cane, his gloves, his coat, his hat, his paper perhaps, to Slater, and the sound of their voices, so different from Selina's, makes a muffled growling sound down below. Sometimes, but not often, it is Rollo home from school who comes in; and the light from the gas in the china globes catches his hair and his tread sounds firm on the hall floor, and his voice, quick and warm and clear, and unmistakably boyish, comes up to Lark's ears. He is as unapproachable as a young god to Lark, and she says over and over all the things he says with that innate lordliness that fills her with admiration and excitement and delight. 'Dash it all Slater—'

'Dash it all Slater—' murmurs Lark.

The Eye and Griselda read: –

'Look,' said Wilfred, reads the Eye. 'There is a cocoanut tree; watch me and I shall soon get you something to drink.' So saying, he climbed up to the tree and drawing his jackknife –

'What is a jackknife?' asks Roly.

'Listen,' says the Eye. And drawing his jackknife he skilfully cut down the fruit and threw it to Francis on the beach below.

And the princess did not sleep a wink, reads Griselda. Not a wink of sleep all night. She tossed and turned and turned and tossed –

'Like this,' says Freddie lifting and bumping himself up and down on his stool.

... and she was bruised black and blue all over. And when she got up in the morning she told the Queen she had not closed an eye all night.

'Like this,' says Freddie. He closes an eye and finds he can only close two, not one by itself.

'Little silly,' says Lena and she scornfully winks and opens in turn each of her jealous pale-blue eyes. 'Look Mamma. *I* can do it,' says Lena.

A new voice speaks on the wireless and this is what Verity has been waiting for. '*. . . and now Juanita Lopez of Montevideo is going to give birthday greetings to Young Listeners who have birthdays to-day, in England. It is Juanita's birthday too of course. She is nine years old to-day. Juanita.*'

'*Hullo everybody,*' says Juanita. '*This is Juanita Lopez of Montevideo speaking to you in the Young Listeners' Friendship League. I wish a happy birthday to Alexander Buckland of Br-righton and to Joanna Jayne of Eastbourne who, like me, are nine to-day; to Constance Mary Ponsonby of Willingham who is eight and to Ger-rald and Ger-raldine White of Ang-mer-ring who also are eight; to . . .*' Verity waits breathlessly while the long long list unfolds.

That other little boy, dark-faced, in the dark serge sailor suit and black socks and shoes, flies upstairs, up from the hall to the landing, from the landing up the second flight, with a blissful incredulous face.

'Dash it Slater,' says Lark under her breath. 'Dash it Slater.'

The Eye and Griselda read on: –

Francis responded by taking out his knife . . .

'Oh I am glad they had one each,' says Roly. 'I was afraid Francis wasn't going to have one.'

. . . and opened the luscious white-fleshed nut.

The Queen was delighted and called everybody in the court to come . . .

Elizabeth, watching Griselda's throat as it rises out of her sapphire-blue dress, gives an enormous yawn.

. . . and said to them, 'This is a real princess.'

'You are getting sleepy,' says Griselda.

Roly seems to catch Elizabeth's yawn.

'You are getting sleepy,' says the Eye.

On the wireless Juanita has worked through the names.

'*And last of all before we say "Good night", gr-reetings to Verity Dane of the gr-reat city of London who is seven years old to-day.*'

Verity gives a whoop of joy. 'You heard Mummie? You heard? That was for me. That was for me.' It is his first public moment. He, his Me, has been publicly recognized.

'*Good night to my fr-riends in England.*'

'*Good night Juanita and thank you. Now Uncle Billy is going to sing.*'

Elizabeth puts her hand over the lump, the small rounded apple in Griselda's throat, and holds it. 'Don't read. Sing,' she commands. 'A song for me, a song for Freddie and one for Lena.'

'And one for Miss Manners,' says Lena. 'I think you have forgotten her.'

> *A ship a ship a-sailing,*
> *A-sailing on the sea . . .*

sings Uncle Billy, and Griselda might easily sing the same song; she sings it often.

> *And oh! it was all laden*
> *With lovely things for me.*

The sky is dark now outside the window.

Uncle Billy has a nutty rollicking voice. Verity listens with his chin on the back of the chair; Verity is a solemn little boy with blue eyes and chestnut hair, the colouring of his great-great-uncle Rolls, of Rollo, of Roly, Elizabeth and Griselda. He is a shade darker than they, but then his father is very dark indeed.

Apples in the cabin,
And toffees in the hold . . .

Again the dark little boy in the dark sailor suit flies upstairs.

The sails were made of satin,
The masts were made of gold.

Griselda's voice is dreamy, her cheek is on Elizabeth's head, and Elizabeth's hand, warm and firm, is on Griselda's throat. 'It feels alive, like a bird in my hand, when you sing,' says Elizabeth.

'It is wrong, very wrong, not to care for your own little children,' Griselda says long ago. 'Someday I shall be punished.'

'My darling love!' the Eye answers her.

It is another evening but no children have come downstairs. The house is hushed, the servants tread differently, the boys and Selina have been sent hastily away, there is straw down in front of the house in the road. The Eye does not go to the office, he waits awkwardly between the study and the stairs, and Griselda is invisible, shut into the nurseries. Dr Flower's greys wait twice or even three times a day; they are there now, down in the street below; the knife boy has been sent out to hold them while Dr Flower's coachman has a mug of porter and a slice of pie in the kitchen.

'Go and lie down,' says Dr Flower to Griselda. 'Nurse and I

are here. You must get some sleep.' And he murmurs all the usual murmurs about conserving strength.

And what shall I do with my strength, asks Griselda, if ... ?

She does not ask it aloud. She prefers not to speak to anyone; in fact she finds it impossible. 'Go and lie down. Sleep.' Obediently she goes.

She is very tired. With stiff hands she takes down her hair that feels heavy and dusty on her head; she realizes that she has not taken it down for two days and nights, not since Freddie ... but she cannot, will not, think about Freddie. With numb fingers she shakes out her hair; she does not look in the glass but she has an impression of white cheeks and haggard hot blue eyes; that may be from the last time she looked in it, two days ago. She unbuttons her bodice, a velvet one, and there are stains down the front of it, from the milk that Freddie pushed away out of her hand. She steps out of her wide heavy-banded skirt that she has worn trailing because the crinoline bumped against the bed. 'You hurt my head,' said a little croaking offended voice. 'I didn't mean to. I wouldn't hurt you my dearest.' She left off the crinoline, and her rustling taffeta petticoat, now she stands in her plain white underslip and winds the Paisley shawl round her and lies down on the couch and pulls the afghan over her feet. While she is straining, listening for a sound upstairs, she is asleep.

'Griselda. Griselda.'

It is Dr Flower running down the stairs, his face shocked. 'Griselda!'

'Doctor!' The children's nurse calls him. 'Doctor! *Doctor!*' she screams and comes running after him to the stairs. He stops and turns and she shakes her head and bursts into tears, stifling her mouth with her apron. They both look at Griselda's door.

Griselda has heard. Even in her exhausted sleep one sense is awake. She is up and out of the door in her shawl, her hair down, her eyes big with fright. They grow more frightened as she sees the nurse, and Dr Flower comes to her down the stairs. 'Is she worse?'

'She is dead.' Dr Flower says it gently, simply and finally.

'But ... she was asleep,' says Griselda. 'I left her asleep. It was – Freddie who died. That was Freddie,' she says urgently. 'That was Freddie. *This* is *Elizabeth*.' She runs past him up the stairs into the nursery.

Elizabeth's hand, as Dr Flower lays it down, lies gently on the bed; it is soft and warm, the fingers curled, a sleeping hand. Her face, when he has bent and closed her eyes, is a sleeping face; her hair lies on the pillow naturally, except for the short ends where they have cut it; her lips are red.

'She is asleep,' says Griselda in a whisper. She touches Elizabeth's fingers. 'She is warm.'

'She was a very sick little girl,' says Dr Flower. 'Now she can rest.'

Griselda slowly stands up. She goes slowly to the window.

In China – in China – when a child dies they take its coat – its coat or a little shoe, some garment, and they run with it out into the street, down the street, everywhere, calling its name. 'Come back. Come back.' Before it is too late they call its name ... Griselda looks up, above the top branches of the plane-tree to the sky where the day is over, where there are points of stars. 'Freddie. Elizabeth. Come back. Come back Elizabeth. Elizabeth come back.'

She begins to weep desperately and painfully. 'I want John,' she cries. 'Oh where is John? I want John. I want John. I want John.'

Grizel was crying on the landing. She cried more quietly than Griselda, but then she was crying for herself.

Rolls, as he came out, changed from the dressing-room, heard her and went to her where she stood disconsolately against the window. 'Why are you crying Grizel?'

He put his arm round her and, as he touched her, emotion surged up in her and she sobbed out, 'I love Pax.'

Rolls's voice was calm. 'Is that something to cry for?'

'Yes it is,' sobbed Grizel fiercely. 'Now I won't know a minute's peace, night or day.'

'Don't be so old for your age,' said Rolls. 'You shouldn't want peace yet.'

'But I do. I have always wanted to be peaceful and tidy and settled, and if I love Pax I can't be any of those things,' wailed Grizel. 'I can't *arrange* anything,' she said indignantly.

'No, you can't arrange it,' agreed Rolls, still calm.

'This hideous hideous war!'

'But that isn't the war,' said Rolls reasonably. 'That is life my dear child, not the war. You can't arrange life. It doesn't let you. I tried,' said Rolls. 'I failed.'

Grizel did not answer. At this moment she was interested solely in herself and Pax. 'I was horrid to Pax just now,' she cried.

'I expect you were,' said Rolls. 'I told you you were a shrew. You are Selina's niece you know.'

Don't keep talking about old people, old people who are dead and gone and useless now. Don't keep on talking as if this were something to do with them. This is Pax and me. Me! Me! Me! cried Grizel silently.

'Good God my God, must you cry again?' said Rolls testily. 'I cheated myself of love. I was a fool. Don't you be a fool. Be young! Be ardent! And don't cry! Don't cry! Don't cry!'

Far above the house, into the quiet night, came the sound of an aeroplane. There was no alert. No gunfire. It was a plane, flying alone. And as it came over the house it made a loud droning that filled their ears.

'You see,' said Grizel.

'Well?' asked Rolls.

'I can't endure it,' said Grizel loudly. 'Maybe other people can, but I can't. It is no use, Uncle Rolls. I have quite decided. I am not going to marry Pax.'

NIGHT

It is night.

There is a moon and because there is no reflected dome of light over the city, the moonlight marks it very plainly; it shows, like a map, roofs and domes and spires and the open spaces of parks, and the gleam of the Thames and the lines of the bridges over it.

The moonlight exposes the whole city to the sky.

Along the walls and up the stairs of Number 99 Wiltshire Place are gilt sconces for candles. Selina keeps them when she puts in gaslight because to remove them means ruining the paper. They have survived and now candles were burning in them, candles in threes, knots of lambent yellow flames up the staircase wall, along the hall and landing, and in the drawing-room.

'Give them candlelight,' said the Marchesa. 'Candles every-where.'

There are degrees of candles. In the beginning, in that green far-off time when the house is first taken, the knife boy who sleeps behind the kitchen is given a dip; and the little scullery maid is given another so that she may come down in the dark morning, her face and body stiff with sleep, to start the fires. There are funeral candles of twisted white wax in huge brass candlesticks supplied by the undertaker to stand at the head and foot of the bed; there are the little gay birthday-cake candles blown out by a ring of children's breaths and there are others, smaller still, shedding their wax quickly on the dark boughs of Christmas trees. There is a candle in the watchman's lantern that burns slowly through the night. It is just the right length to last it through.

Griselda often hears the watchman. She often lies awake after her John, tired and healthily satisfied, has fallen asleep. Griselda is glad, happy, that she satisfies him; she is proud of the completeness of her hold on him; and yet, mingled with this and her own joy, and sometimes it is joy though sometimes it is near repulsion, is scorn of John, of the Eye, for being so easily satisfied. You think you have me, Griselda might have said, but you don't. You only have a part of me and afterwards John I am strangely more inaccessible to you than before.

She lies awake. She hears the watchman. 'Ten o'clock. All's well.'

She thinks again of travelling. The rivers of China. She sees herself on a river with yellow water between banks of rice-fields where Chinese cultivators and Chinese egrets are at work; the cultivators work at their rice crops, the egrets at catching insects; the cultivators wear blue clothes, great circular straw hats; the egrets wear slim feathers, dazzling white. I am sailing in a junk, says Griselda, but the word *junk* brings her back abruptly to the bazaar at the Guildhall she is helping with next day. A sigh escapes into the darkness but she makes no movement that would disturb the Eye, wake John beside her. The Eye lies peacefully, sleeping confidently and well. Griselda looks into the darkness. She would like to think of that far river but she thinks instinctively of the near bazaar.

'Eleven o'clock,' calls the watchman. 'All's well.'

Griselda faints at dinner one night years later. When Dr Flower arrives, he finds the Eye pacing the hall in apprehension and indignation. 'She has never done such a thing before,' says the Eye. 'She has come round but she isn't herself. She asked me to leave her alone!'

'Hm!' says Dr Flower. 'Hmm?' He looks at the Eye over the wing-tips of his high immaculate starched collar. 'I think you owe me a glass of port, John, fetching me out at this time of night. Go into the study and I shall join you.'

Dr Flower goes into the drawing-room. Griselda is lying on a couch, her head turned away, her eyes shut.

'Well Griselda.'

She does not move. She says with her eyes still shut: 'They needn't have sent for you. I am sorry.'

He sits down by her and feels her pulse. 'Tell me,' he says.

She opens her eyes and tries to smile at him but it is only a bitter little half-smile and it disappears. 'It is about three months,' she says. 'I tried to think it wasn't true, but you see it is. It will be born at the beginning of December.'

Dr Flower has never seen Griselda look so plain; she is still wearing black; for three years she has worn black, and in her pallor, with dark liverish patches under her eyes and her hair dulled and heavy, she looks lifeless. He questions her and she sits with her hands clasped tightly so that the knuckles and wrists are white. 'It will be born in December,' she says.

'I am glad about it,' says little Dr Flower. 'I am glad about it Griselda. It will replace those other two.'

Freddie and – Elizabeth were people, Griselda cries fiercely, you don't replace people! But she cries it silently: she does not contradict Dr Flower. She stands up and goes to the fire because she is very cold. 'Stupid to faint. To bring you out so late,' she says.

'I am going to take you into the study now,' says Dr Flower, 'John has a glass of wine.'

'I don't want a glass of wine.' She holds out her hands to the fire and the firelight lights the edges of them and makes them look sensitive and thin as the electric glow made Pax's. 'I don't think I want to see John just now,' says Griselda slowly.

'What is it Griselda?'

'Dr Flower, you must have seen hundreds of babies: brought them into the world as you did ours. How can you go on being so hopeful about each one?'

'I don't know,' says Dr Flower. 'But I am.'

'Are you? Can you be?'

'Yes,' says Dr Flower. 'You think that is sentimental, don't you Griselda?'

'I think it is silly,' says Griselda. 'How – funny to be hopeful about Elizabeth and Freddie who promised so much and lived five years and died in pain; about boys who grow up and turn into soldiers and kill other boys and die themselves, wiped out, just when they should have flowered; 'the flower of English manhood', that is what they call it, don't they? About factory children, and those little girls and boys who worked in the mines, those children Lord Ashley fought for; and little girls who grow up into maids and are shut up all their lives to work in a house like this; about their mistresses treading the little treadmill like a squirrel in a cage, round and round so that it will turn round all over again. You must be extraordinarily hopeful Dr Flower.'

'I am,' says Dr Flower.

'How can you be?'

'Because,' says Dr Flower firmly, his pink cheeks rising out of his collar-tips above his snow-white stock, his white hair shining, 'because I believe it will be ultimately just.'

'Just? But it is wickedly unjust.'

'Now, yes. Ultimately not.'

'How could it be? How could it possibly be?'

'It is too giant for us to understand,' says Dr Flower. 'But in the end we shall be satisfied.'

'You believe that?' says Griselda and again she says, 'How – funny. How separated we all are. You and I, in this room.' And she says to the fire, 'I believe in nothing at all' – and in the same moment she cries, 'Giant! Yes. It crushes all us little things.' And then she says clearly and without any drama, 'This time it is going to kill me.'

'You are being foolish and cowardly Griselda,' says Dr Flower. 'Very foolish and very cowardly. It is a purely natural process.'

'I wish doctors had purely natural processes,' says Griselda with that bitter little smile. 'Then they might do something about the purely natural pain. Oh well—' she says and then she cries: 'But it isn't the pain, nor the ugliness, nor the trap—'

'The trap, Griselda?'

'Yes, the trap. I am sick of them Dr Flower. I am sick and tired of your giant and your men. I am tired. Tired. Tired.'

'And so I was born here, nearly eighty years ago,' Rolls was telling Pax and Grizel as he went before them down the stairs. 'I – the Me I know came into being.' And he added to himself, That I is very valuable to me. I should hate it to be lost. He looked at Grizel as she caught him up and came down beside him, and he hoped that she would marry this slim dark, somehow notable young man. In spite of her protests, he thought that she would. 'Grizel . . . ' he said.

She stopped, looked up at him, and he thought how much he liked her face with its clear skin and straight small nose, the pretty mouth, the direct blue eyes and well-brushed fine brown hair. 'Yes Uncle Rolls?' But he said nothing to her after all. What is the use? he said to himself. Why worry? To-morrow we must go.

'I had the whole house very nearly right,' said Pax in that moment. 'But now it is all crystallized in my mind. Thank you for taking us over it.' He looked round as they came into the drawing-room. 'There is a crystal quality about the house this evening,' he said, 'as if this were the moment. No,' he corrected himself, 'as if all the moments were crystallized in this.'

'How could they be?' said Grizel crossly.

'Stop wrangling,' said Rolls, and he went on, speaking to Pax: 'There is a poem; I found it a few days ago and it stays in my head. Listen: –

> Home is where one starts from. As we grow older
> The world becomes stranger, the pattern more complicated
> Of dead and living. Not the intense moment
> Isolated, with no before and after,
> But a lifetime burning in every moment
> And not the lifetime of one man only

But of old stones that cannot be deciphered,
There is a time for the evening under starlight,
A time for the evening under lamplight
(The evening with the photograph album).
Love is most nearly itself
When here and now cease to matter.
Old men ought to be explorers
Here or there does not matter
We must be still and still moving
Into another intensity
For a further union, a deeper communion . . .
. . . In my end is my beginning.'

'I didn't think of you and poetry, Uncle Rolls,' said Grizel.
'Didn't you?' Rolls's smile was tender and pitiful and a little envious as he looked down on her cross miserable face. 'There are several things you don't think of yet, Grizel.' And he said: 'Wait here. I have something I want to give you, for our last night. It is in the safe upstairs. I shall be a few minutes.'

When he had gone Grizel moved away from Pax to the fire and stood with her back to him warming her hands.

'You have been delightfully cross all evening,' said Pax pleasantly.

'I wish you would go away.'

'Why?'

'You know why. Do we have to start arguing all over again?'

'I am afraid we do,' said Pax.

'You have turned me into a worse coward than I used to be.' Her voice was shaking. 'I tell you I can't bear it. I don't want to be attached or concerned or intimate.'

'Selfish little beast.'

'Yes I am selfish. I want to be. I want to be like those people who come through a war without a scratch.'

'No one comes through a war without a scratch; not this war anyway,' said Pax. 'You can't, so why go to all this trouble to try?'

'Ever since I arrived, ever since I came to this house, everything has made one long attack on me.'

'Well, why should you escape?' asked Pax unsympathetically, and he said seriously, his eyes bright, 'No one is going to escape this time.'

'Judgement Day?' asked Grizel flippantly.

'If you like.'

'Armageddon? And we shall all become the images of Christ?'

'Christ was a model of what can be done,' said Pax and his voice was light and certain. 'You see I can only believe that Christ started evenly; even as we are. I don't think anyway it is necessary to believe he was born divine. I think that is optional. He became divine,' and he said quietly, 'That is why I think they are right when they call him the hope of the world.'

'I do nothing but cry,' said Grizel angrily.

'Why? There is nothing to cry about.'

She squeezed her handkerchief between her hands. 'Why? Why? Look at me now. I am starting again.' She bit her lips but the tears ran down her cheeks. 'I am a mediocre person,' she said angrily. 'I didn't ask for heroics. I only want to be comfortable and enjoy myself.'

'Then why did you come here? This is a country fighting for

its life,' said Pax mildly. 'Didn't you expect it to be heroic and uncomfortable?'

'I expected it to be exciting,' said Grizel defiantly through her tears.

'No my darling,' said Pax. 'You are not as young as that.' He came to her and put his arm round her and held her. 'Why not be truthful Grizel? You love me and I love you. That is the truth isn't it?'

Grizel nodded dumbly and her tears dropped on to his hand.

'And there is nothing we can do to stop it is there,' said Pax, 'however much we try?'

'Nothing we can do,' said Grizel. 'But . . .'

'Kiss me,' said Pax.

She put her arms round his neck and kissed him with her whole heart. 'Oh Pax, I love you. I love you so much but it is silly, stupid, to be vulnerable and hopeful now. Talk to me Pax. Help me. Comfort me.'

'Things are serious just now,' said Pax with his cheek against hers. 'You have to treat them seriously but it is of no use to be afraid. I should be afraid if it made us any safer, but it doesn't. You have to think, I think, that anything we do in any time, the smallest thing, like ordering the paper to come every day or promising to go out to dinner next Wednesday week, or getting a new tube of toothpaste, particularly the large size that lasts twice as long, is an act of faith. It is an act of faith to think or hope or plan, but I intend to go on doing it. There are dozens of things I want. I intend to go on as if I shall get them all.'

'What are they Pax? What do you want?'

'You first. I want to be married at once. Then I want a child. Immediately.'

'Are you – so fond of children?' asked Grizel doubtfully.

'Only of my own,' said Pax. 'Yes. I want a child. I want to make quite sure of that while I am here on earth.'

'Don't Pax.'

'It is only an act of faith,' said Pax. 'And whether it is a boy or a girl, I want us to call it Verity.'

'Verity,' said Grizel sounding it and testing it. She liked it. 'But he won't live here in this house,' she said regretfully.

'Then in a house like it,' answered Pax, 'if he can't live here. But you never know Grizel. I feel he will live here. Here and at Laudi. That would be a link.'

'All the new children ought to be links,' said Grizel. 'He would link us all up. Link Lark and Rolls again through you and me. Shall we tell Rolls?'

'No,' said Pax slowly. 'I don't think so. I shouldn't disturb it now.'

The door opened and Rolls came back into the room. He had a small leather case in his hand. 'I wanted to give you this Grizel,' he said. 'To-night.'

Grizel looked at his face. He seemed rapt away from them so that he did not really notice them nor see what she was sure was an alteration in their faces; he did not see that they stood in front of him hand in hand, or if he did, it seemed to him so natural, as it seemed to her now, that it called for no remark.

'To-night is important,' said Grizel slowly. It was to-night that had made her speak in this new tender voice, effulgent with tenderness.

'To-night is our last night and you and Pax dined with me,' said Rolls. 'Isn't that enough?'

'It is enough,' said Grizel judiciously, 'but it isn't all.'

From the front door a bell rang through the house.

'Proutie is out on duty to-night,' said Rolls moving towards the door.

'Wait. I will go,' Grizel ran past him. They heard her open the door and heard voices and then she came slowly back along the hall.

'It is a telegram, for Pax.'

'For me? But nobody knows I am here.'

'Somebody does,' said Grizel, holding it out to him. 'It is for you.'

Pax took it and slowly opened it. He read it with his back to them in a silence and when at last he spoke his voice was high and nervously light and he looked at Rolls. 'It has come through Switzerland. From Geneva,' he said. 'It is from my cousin. I – am sorry sir—'

'Lark?' asked Rolls.

Pax nodded. For a moment he could not speak and he bent and stirred the fire and beat in a piece of coal. Presently he stood up again and said: 'She died last month. Before I came here, she was dead.' And then he turned back to Rolls. 'You knew,' he said. 'You knew.'

'I didn't know,' Rolls answered. 'I guessed.' He took Pax gently by the shoulder and turned him from the fire. 'I think,' he said, 'this is the time that you and Grizel should go out dancing.'

'Dancing. *Now?*' asked Grizel.

'Yes.'

'No, Uncle Rolls.'

'Yes. Quite apart from any other reason I want you to leave me please. Pax wants you Grizel. Wait though. There is something else. Two other things. I found this when I went upstairs.'

He showed them a letter. 'I had forgotten to open it, but I answered it at once. I answered it,' he said, 'but it concerns you. It will concern you, not myself.' He gave the letter to Pax not to Grizel. 'He will be the head of the house I hope,' he said. 'You won't let her rule, will you Pax?' Pax read the letter, still holding the telegram in his hand.

'Willoughby is young Willoughby of my solicitors,' said Rolls. 'A conceited useless young man I consider, but this time it seems that he has been of use.'

Grizel read the letter over Pax's shoulder . . . *After a great deal of correspondence and several interviews . . . the owners . . . changes of circumstances and present conditions . . . the difficulty of getting materials and labour . . . am delighted to be able to inform you . . . the house is now for sale, subject to the . . . if you . . .*

'For sale! We can buy it,' cried Grizel. 'Oh Uncle Rolls! But can you buy it? Will you?'

'I have,' said Rolls. 'This is the answer and the cheque is in it. Here it is. You can post it on your way to-night.' He gave the envelope to Pax. 'In return you can leave me that.' And gently he took the telegram from Pax's hand and put it in his waistcoat pocket. 'The house,' he said, 'is to belong to you.'

'Why Uncle Rolls! To us and you. Ours,' said Grizel. 'Forever.'

'It is only a lease of occupation, mind,' said Rolls.

'But you said . . . you have *bought* it, Uncle Rolls.'

'I have bought it,' said Rolls. 'But don't you forget that, Grizel.'

'We thought it was going to end after to-night,' said Grizel, 'and it isn't. It is going to live.'

Rolls looked down at her then over her head at Pax. 'Do you subscribe to that?' he asked.

'Yes. I do,' said Pax and again he gave to little words their greatest weight.

'Then you can leave me with a quiet conscience,' said Rolls. He opened the case he held and put it into Grizel's hand.

'Pearls,' said Grizel. 'Oh! Uncle Rolls!'

'Pearls,' he chuckled. 'They are a small string but perfectly matched. You won't get a string like that in a hurry,' he boasted. 'I gave them to Lark. I kept them because ...Well, you must have them now Grizel. I gave them to her on her birthday.' He chuckled again. 'I was determined to go one better than Pelham. You didn't know, did you, Grizel, that your grandfather was in love with Lark? He gave her a bracelet. The shops were shut when I found that out but I made them open one for me. I knew the fellow. I had bought odds and ends from him before and he had shown me these. He didn't think that I could buy them though. There was nothing there to touch them. They cost me every penny I had and I had to sell Mousetrap, my best pony. But you should have seen Pelham's face when he saw them! And Selina's!'

'And Lark's,' said Grizel softly.

The boasting and the glee went out of him. 'Oh well,' he said and there was something humble and gentle in his voice. 'She wore them for one night and then she gave them back to me.'

'Was she very angry?' The pearls looked up at Grizel, a string of translucent separate little moons on their pale velvet.

'It was of no use to be angry,' said Rolls. 'It was my doing, but I suppose you might just as well have said to a puppy "Don't breathe." Yes a puppy,' said Rolls and he sounded angry now. 'A conceited, selfish, self-engrossed young puppy.'

A puppy? Yes. That, thought Grizel, was what they often called a young man, as they called a woman a cat. A young young man; but where, she wondered, had that quality gone? How singularly unlike puppies were the young men she now knew; how unlike a puppy, for instance, was Pax. Rollo, then, must have been many years older than Pax. Have young men grown older then? she asked. Are they now more human? Have they achieved humanity? Are they not now, as they used often to seem to be, not puppies but half cardboard creatures, half animal? In Rolls's time the animal was not allowed to be mentioned, was that why only the cardboard seemed to remain? Looking back, judging by what she had heard, she seemed to see Rollo as stiff, conventional and powerless. Not a blood. Not a blood but a blade. She looked at him now and she asked, 'What about you now Uncle Rolls?'

'For years I was too busy to remember,' his words came forcefully into the quiet of the room. 'I was too busy to think. She, Lark, the Marchesa, was busy too. Then she had long hours to spend alone. So had I. That is all.' And he smiled. 'All there is to tell. She used to say we should have six children and a million pounds a year. Well, it isn't quite like that. It couldn't be. But we don't want anything else.' And he said to Grizel, 'Put on the pearls.'

Pax came up behind her and lifted the pearls from the case and put them round her neck and fastened the clasp. 'Say "Good night", Grizel,' he said. 'We are going now.'

She reached up and kissed Rolls and he bent down to her and kissed her on the mouth. Her lips clung to his and she tightened her hand on his arm. 'Good night.'

'Good night Grizel. Good night Pax.'

'Good night. Good night.'

They left him and went out and shut the door. Presently he heard the front door close.

The room was still.

'Have those two children gone?'

'Just gone. I get days – and particularly nights – of being afraid for Pax,' said Rolls.

'It is funny,' said the Marchesa. 'When he was little he had great sad eyes like an owl, fearfully wise. Now he is big his eyes have gone little and merry and bright.'

'They are wise all the same,' said Rolls. 'I used to call him "the Interloper". I don't feel he is an interloper now.'

'An interloper? When I used to make him fly upstairs? Oh, poor Pax. He used to love that game and to hear about the house. I remembered everything for him.'

'Do you remember everything now?'

'Not everything. Things change. Things that we thought were little, have become big; big ones, little; like Pax's eyes. Some things I remember are such absurd irrelevant things. I remember a forget-me-not wreath. Why?' said the Marchesa. 'I never had one.'

'Wait. What is the name of a flower—' said Rolls suddenly – 'It has two names, one easy and one difficult. A knot of little flowers, deep purple. They are the first thing I remember. They have a very fragrant smell.'

'Heliotrope, and they call it cherry-pie.'

'I knew you would know.' He sat down with a contented sigh. 'I never had time for flowers except through you. I think of you and flowers. I am sick of belligerent women,' said Rolls.

'The candles are burning down,' said the Marchesa.

'That dress you wore, that night, our night – what was it made of?' asked Rolls.

'But I told you.'

Clearly into the night outside came the sound of an alert and a moment after, far off, the beginning of the guns.

Rollo asks the same question as Rolls. 'What is that dress made of?'

'But I told you,' says Lark.

'Tell me again. No you needn't. I know. It shines as if it were not there. It is called illusion.'

'Silly. Our grandmothers wore illusion.'

'Is there a real stuff called illusion? You didn't mind coming home Lark? Missing those last dances?'

'No. Did you?'

'No.'

They have come home to talk. 'Let us get away from here. I want to talk to you Lark. I must be alone with you, for a little while I must.' Now they are here, alone together, they can neither of them say a word they mean.

Lark is sitting on the arm of one of the red chairs, her dress spread round her. Rollo stands by the fire, one elbow on the mantelpiece, one leg, in its shining breech and boot, balanced on the fender rail. The gas is not lit, but Slater has left candles burning in the sconces above the piano and each side of the mantelpiece. They shine down on Rollo's hair, reddening its chestnut, making it gleam. Lark looks at his hair.

'You are not tired?' he asks again. 'You don't want to go to bed?' He knows perfectly well she does not want to go to bed.

'No. Do you?' She knows equally well that he does not either.

'No.'

'Pelham was tired,' says Lark. Are they, she wonders, to go on talking of being tired forever? To go wandering round and round in these circles that are so very far from the way they mean to take? Then Rollo lifts his head.

'Do you always kiss Pelham good night? Does he kiss you?'

'When Pelham kisses me,' says Lark dreamily, 'it doesn't go any deeper than my skin.' She feels now as if she were speaking in a dream, but it is real at last. Rollo takes his elbow off the mantelpiece.

'And when I kiss you?' asks Rollo and his voice, as once before, is blurred and husky.

There is a sudden stillness.

'You have never kissed me – yet.'

Then Lark, as if she were compelled to, deliberately puts a spoke into this wheel that is turning so dazzlingly towards her. It might be called a Catherine wheel of hope and fear, bright as flames and sparks, but she arrests it. She says, 'I keep thinking of India.'

Rollo is jerked abruptly to a standstill. 'Why do you want to think of that now?'

'I don't want to. I have to,' says Lark and she goes deeper deliberately though she hurts herself. 'I think of it, and you, and of myself. It will be exciting for you of course. Think of all the things you will see: wild animals and queer flowers; queer religions; the Taj Mahal and Fatehpur Sikri and the Ganges and crocodiles. I can see you Rollo,' she says sadly, 'on a pony under a palm. You have been playing polo I expect. I see a minaret, and a peacock.' And she catches her breath as she says, 'Of course India is very gay.'

'Need you say that?' he says angrily. 'Need you tease me now?'

'What else can I do?' She stands up and comes so close to him, by the fire, that her eyes are on a level with his face, and he can smell the scent on her skin and on her hair and the fire-light on her dress. Her eyes are dark with feeling, her lips have stopped laughing and he can see her throat move as if words welled up in it, but she does not speak. He does not speak either but he puts out his hand as if he would take hers. 'Don't touch me,' whispers Lark. 'Please Rollo, please don't touch me.'

He says with a helpless groan, 'Oh Lark! Oh Lark! What can we do?'

She turns her head and he bends his and before they know what they are doing they have kissed. Lark gives a little sob and tries to take her lips away but Rollo holds her to him. 'I love you Lark. I love you,' he says with his lips against hers. 'How much I love you Lark.'

When he lifts his head, Lark stands against him unutterably happy even though in her happiness there is a quality of surprise. She leans against him, feeling his arms round her, and she looks down into the fire and round the room. The room is still the same; the candles are burning quietly along the walls; they shine on the gold in the barley-sheaves and poppies in the paper, on the picture frames, on the gilding of the chairs exactly as they did before; they are reflected quietly in the polished piano lid, in the tables, in the mirror; none of them have burst into torches; the shepherdess on the clock is still dreaming and the hands of the clock have only imperceptibly moved; the bronze chrysanthemums in the Chinese bowls are as they were: they have not hung themselves in garlands nor in wreaths; but 'Then?' says Lark wonderingly. 'Then? And now?' She murmurs: 'I can't believe it is true. Is it true?'

'It is true,' says Rollo.

'We shall have six children and a million pounds a year.'

'What did you say Lark?'

'Nothing.' She shuts her eyes and feels his strength behind her. 'I was thinking.'

He looks down, watching her lashes against her cheek. 'What are you thinking of?'

'Of us of course.'

'How we shall always be in love?'

'How we shall always be in love.'

'Even when we are old?'

'Even when we are old.'

'What made us say that?' asked the Marchesa. 'What made us choose that to say?'

'And then Selina came in,' said Rolls. 'She was always good at cooking other people's geese for them.'

'It was your own goose,' said the Marchesa.

The door opens and Selina comes in. Rolo and Lark cannot help it, they spring apart like guilty children.

Selina has come in full of triumph: her face is lit by it. Her dress of black gauze over taffeta rustles importantly into the room and the candles pick up the fire of her rubies, the ruby set she inherited from Griselda and that Griselda was given by the Eye. She rustles in full of triumph and she stops suspended on a rustle and gleam, as she sees Lark in Rollo's arms. Her face hardens into an icy coldness.

The sight of visible tenderness is at any time abominable to Selina, but the sight of Rollo and Lark makes her feel as if she were struck and turned to ice. For a minute she stands petrified and then on a wave of angry disgust she comes forward. Lark, after she has sprung away, goes back to Rollo and puts her hand into his, and Selina sees her little finger, as she faces her, caressing and caressing Rollo's hand. Rollo moves closer to Lark and puts his shoulder behind hers and bends his cheek quietly, privately, to feel her hair. Violent words seethe up in Selina, but by an extraordinary effort she does not say them: she says nothing at all but turns from the sight of them to take off her gloves beside the piano.

'Well,' says Rollo like a dangerous bull.

'Well, Rollo, I congratulate you,' says Selina lightly.

'*Congratulate* me?' Lark and Rollo stare at her.

'Yes. It is all settled.'

'What – is all settled?' But Rollo knows. A dual set of feelings rise up in him, excitement and a gratified pleasure, and with them, a defiant obstinacy against Selina and them all.

'My dear boy!' The glove buttons, not being made of iron but of delicate mother-of-pearl, betray Selina; one of them is jerked off and flies across the carpet to Lark's feet. 'Uncle Bunny saw Lord Fitzgerald last night. He will be taking you to call there to-morrow at eleven, but that is only a formality. It is settled and it will be confirmed. I must say you are very lucky Rollo. What an adventure! Uncle Bunny is so delighted.'

'What is it you have accepted for Rollo?'

That is from Lark. Selina moves to put her gloves down ignoring the question but Lark's voice cuts across her, 'Answer me please.'

Selina looks at Lark, as if she were measuring her. She says coldly: 'Rollo is to be on the staff of Lord Fitzgerald, who has been lent to Afghanistan on a special mission to take over the Army there and remodel it. Lord Fitzgerald fought at Char-asiab and Kabul and Kandahar – what names to stir you Rollo – and he was asked for by the present Amir. It is a wonderful opportunity for Rollo. They sail on the *Hindustan* next week, going overland to Marseilles.'

'Next week!'

'It is dreadfully soon of course,' say Selina's lips. Not a moment too soon, say her eyes, jealous quick eyes that cannot help watching that finger. Now she sees Rollo's hand close over it, stilling it, as he crushes Lark's hand in his.

'Lark and I love one another,' he says defiantly to Selina. 'We are going to be married.'

Selina is not often wise in her dealings with Rollo but now she is instilled with an insidious serpentine wisdom. 'You can be married of course,' she says. 'You can wait five years.'

'Five years.' Lark seems powerless to do anything but repeat Selina's words.

'The appointment under the Afghan government is for five years,' says Selina and she sees Lark's eyes, startled and frightened.

'I can't wait five years,' says Lark. 'Selina knows I can't.'

'I refuse to go,' says Rollo.

Selina curbs herself. 'You can refuse of course,' she agrees. 'You have to decide that for yourself, but of course if you did that at the eleventh hour, it would rather reflect on you wouldn't it? Uncle Bunny, for instance, wouldn't be pleased. You have to remember too that it is more than just an appointment; it is an exceptional chance. How many people, Rollo, get a chance to see a country like that? Almost unknown, full of adventure and romance. And you will, if of course you go, be working with a great man. Lord Fitzgerald is a great soldier.

You will get your majority too. Think of it. A major at twenty-seven!'

Rollo looks at her and he cannot help smiling. Lark sees that smile.

'The Duke of Wellington was a colonel at twenty-four,' says Lark.

Rollo's smile fades. He looks hostile.

'If Rollo plays his cards well—'

'I thought he was a soldier, not a card player.'

'You are being silly,' says Rollo sharply.

'Of course, if you refuse to go, you can be married,' says Selina, 'but what will you live on? You can't live on your pay. A captain's pay isn't a great deal you know, and you are only just a captain. For years you would have to scrape along. You haven't any money, have you Lark?'

Lark looks at her with dread and with dislike.

'After five years things should be very different,' says the wily Selina. 'It is only five years.'

Rollo is perfectly still behind Lark.

'She knows that I can't wait five years,' says Lark. 'That is why she suggests it. She knows I can't.' And she cries in desperation, 'She hates me and Pelham is in love with me and it is intolerable for me here. I can't wait Rollo. Don't listen to her. Don't be afraid. She means to spoil it and cut it short. Don't let her Rollo. Don't be afraid. Let us marry and be together and manage our lives for ourselves. I am not afraid. Let us trust ourselves. Rollo listen. Listen to me.'

'I think Rollo would regret it,' says Selina.

It is Selina's calmness and her understatement that wins Rollo; it has the effect of sounding wise, and Lark's vivid eager speech sounds improbable; and she gives herself away to him over and over again, and he knows, or he thinks he knows, that he is safe in arming himself against her for the present. She will wait, thinks Rollo and aloud he says: 'Lark. Listen to me. Dearest I love you—'

Lark looks into his face. 'Second-best love,' says Lark slowly, drawing herself away.

'It has to be second,' says Rollo with a curious honesty. 'But I love you Lark. You must trust me.'

She cries, 'How can I? I know that look, that Dane look in your eyes.'

'I shall marry you when I come back,' says Rollo.

'Will you?' asks Lark with an edge to her voice.

'I promise you I will.'

'Thank you,' says Lark. 'And if I am not here when you come back?'

'You are making things impossible for me,' says Rollo angrily.

'And you are making things impossible for me,' says Lark quietly.

'It is too late . . .'

'It isn't too late.'

'Lark, don't you see, I have to go.'

'If you have to, you have to. It is for you to decide.'

'Lark . . .'

'If you have to, you have to,' says Lark. 'But you can't expect me to agree.'

'Lark. Promise me you will wait.'

'I haven't decided, I haven't decided,' says Lark in a faraway little voice, proud and jerky and broken. 'I haven't decided yet what I shall do.'

'Lark. Listen . . .'

'It is no use to listen,' says Lark proudly, 'I have heard.'

'Will you be reasonable?'

'It isn't a question of reason. It is feeling,' says Lark. 'I can't help it, can I, if you have more reason than I have, and I have more feeling than you?'

'It is impossible to talk to you.'

'Why talk then? It is settled. You have settled it, completely, haven't you? You had settled it all the time. Why go on making excuses?'

'I am *not* making excuses!'

Rollo spins round furiously to the mantelpiece. Lark is still, withdrawn from him to the other side of the fire, drawing a circle in the hearthrug with the toe of her white slipper, holding the mantelpiece with one hand, the other caught in the loop of his pearls, twisting them in her fingers.

'You will break them,' says Rollo suddenly.

Lark lifts both her hands and undoes the clasp and drops the necklace on the mantelpiece.

'What a noise we were making just then,' she says.

'Lark, what are you going to do?'

'I told you, I haven't decided.'

'What do you mean?'

'I haven't decided,' repeated Lark. 'But I don't think I shall wait for you, Rollo.'

'Lark you are angry now . . .'

'No I am not angry,' says Lark, and then the unreality in her voice breaks and she comes back to the real moment and she cries, hiding her face in her hands, 'But don't you see, we shall be lost! Lost!'

'But I didn't cry for you Rolls,' said the Marchesa. 'Griselda's tears are in this house, and Grizel's, but not mine. I didn't cry for you. I wouldn't. I have always refused to be unhappy.'

'Unhappy? Happy? I don't know,' said Rolls. The gunfire was getting nearer. Now the house shook. He listened to the guns. 'But we didn't live – not as we might have done. That was my fault.'

'Mine too,' said the Marchesa. 'I was proud.'

'We deserve to end,' said Rolls.

'There are Pax and Grizel,' she reminded him. 'We are not alone.'

And long ago, from a Christmas night, the carol singers begin: –

> *God rest you merry gentlemen,*
> *Let nothing you dismay . . .*

The singing comes from outside in the Place, up to the landing where Selina is sitting alone. Her guests have gone, though like an echo Mr Baldrick's 'Ha!' seems to ring in the hall and up the stairs. The little tree stands where Proutie has left it, its last candle carefully put out, its branches dull. Selina, an old old lady, sits in her armchair with Juno at her feet, and looks at it.

> *O tidings of comfort and joy . . .*

I was sentimental, says Selina looking at the tree.

Behind the tree the house seems cavernous. There is no one in it but the servants and Juno and Selina.

And with true love and brotherhood
Each other now embrace.
This holy tide of Christmas
Is drawing on apace.
O tidings of comfort and joy.

'Come Juno,' says Selina as she slowly stands up. 'Come Juno. We will go to bed.'

And with Juno waddling behind her, she goes through the silent empty house to her own room.

Rolls moved his chair farther away from the window. The glass rattled now to the guns. The candles were getting low. One of them began to gutter. 'Were you afraid to die?' he asked the Marchesa. 'Were you prepared?'

'We are always prepared more or less,' said the Marchesa judiciously. 'Death comes every minute. Guido took a long time dying and they were always exhorting him to prepare for death, but in the end he was much as usual. Your death is a part of your life,' said the Marchesa to Rolls.

He went to the shelf of little books over the writing table – Griselda's books, Selina's books – and took down a prayer-book so much used that it almost fell apart in his hand. He turned the flimsy pages over until he came to page 192: 'The Order for the Burial of the Dead'. If I am found reading this, said Rolls, how suitable that will be!

Man that is born of a woman hath but a short time to live . . .
He cometh up, and is cut down, like a flower; he fleeth as it were a shadow, and never continueth in one stay.

Rolls was not a poet but he knew what it feels like to be a poet and in this critical suspense – the noise outside was hideous – he could be stirred to pleasure.

In the midst of life we are in death ... Well, that was commonly known; the Marchesa, Lark, had pointed that out just now; but there was a line later that arrested him, and for a moment, grimly. 'We shall be lost! Lost.' Lark's cry rang in his ear. *The bitter pangs of eternal death*, read Rolls; and then into his mind came the thought of Grizel. He thought how much he liked her face with its clear skin and straight small nose, the pretty mouth, the direct blue eyes and well-brushed fine brown hair. 'We thought it was going to end, after to-night. And it isn't. It is going to live,' said Grizel. 'Do you subscribe to that?' asked Rolls now of Pax. 'Yes I do,' said Pax, the slim dark, somehow notable young man. 'Yes I do,' said Pax.

Ashes to ashes and dust to dust, Rolls read calmly. He was calm now. 'Are we dust when we die?' asks Roly. Rolls read to the end of the service, quite calm, quite undisturbed.

The heading on the opposite page caught his eye. 'The Thanksgiving of Women after Child-birth'. He remembered now that one followed after the other.

Children and the fruit of the womb are an heritage and gift ... Like as the arrows in the hand of the giant: even so are the young children ...

Arrows, thought Rolls, and he went to the windows, the French doors, and, holding the book still in his hand, carefully, without disturbing the folds of the curtains, he slipped between them and the glass to look out. The raid was drawing nearer;

the sky was not dark but radiant with moonlight, and the crossed patterns and beams of searchlights, moving, crossing, fixing; the air was a heavy pandemonium of sound. Close to him the windows shook and the floor under his feet shook too as if train after train were running underneath. But the trains are stopped, thought Rolls helplessly. He was frightened though he still possessed that undisturbed deep inner calm. *Arrows in the hand of the giant*, thought Rolls.

Well, I have shot my bolt now, thought Rolls as the noise unfolded itself across the sky and seemed to gather and thunder over his head. I am ready. I was born almost eighty years ago. It is fair, and he wondered why he had been afraid. Your death is a part of your life. Heads and tails on a coin that you spin every day; any day; not only this day. To be born and to live and to die is quite usual. Perfectly fair.

He steadied himself by the window and watched the searchlights that hid the stars completely by their near brightness. The whole sky and the city were fraught with death and life.

If he pressed his face against the glass – Highly dangerous, thought Rolls automatically – but if he stayed there he could see the plane-tree. I am that tree, thought Rolls but he flattered himself. It was more than he, as was the other tree of which he truly was a part, the tree drawn on parchment that hung in the hall.

An aeroplane swooped down closer, so close that it sounded as if it swooped down across the garden. Rolls could not see it, only hear, in the lit darkness, that deafening swoop; the gunfire that followed it seemed to crack in his ears, and there was a deafening shock and the house shook again, the glass rattled loudly and Rolls covered his eyes. Then came a lull and he could hear his own breathing. He uncovered his eyes and now in front of him he could see a glare behind the roofs and chimneys opposite. Near, said Rolls. Edward's Square I should think. I hope Proutie is all right.

There is something that no one knows in the house except Rolls himself and Proutie. It is so long ago that Rolls now did not know if Proutie remembered it, but Proutie did remember.

It is Rollo's last night before he leaves for India and Afghanistan, across France to Marseilles, with old Fitzgerald. Rollo is used to going away; since he went away to school for the first time he has been going away continuously; he has almost always been away; then why suddenly should he mind? Mind, care, grieve, yes grieve over this going away. Why cannot he be gay and light and casual as he has always been before? Has always been reproached for being before? He cannot. He is miserable and sulky and, when at last the interminable last evening is over and he goes up to bed, he cannot go to bed; he comes downstairs again and flings the front door open and stands on the steps, and presently he goes outside and spends an hour walking, walking, up and down. It is a cold night and he has no coat but he does not notice that except for a slight extra unconscious misery that comes from being chilled. The sky is light enough to see the shape of the spire, the convent cross; and the street lamps shine, each with a blue and yellow gas-jet; they throw his shadow, shaped not unlike a spire itself, before and then behind him as he walks. Before, behind, before, goes the shadow. The fronts of the houses are bland and indifferent, all with dark windows, and an overmastering desire comes to Rollo to see if Her window is dark; if She can sleep. He goes down by the area steps into the garden.

The plane-tree reaches to the window he is seeking, hiding it, but he can see that behind the branches there is no gleam of light. Rollo goes back into the Place. 'If she can sleep, then I can too,' but he begins to walk up and down again; before, behind, before, goes the shadow.

Rollo is still haunted by his vision. He has eschewed it, torn it in pieces, cast it out, deliberately had nothing to do with it – and it still persists. It still comes back again: the garden, the trees, the flight of steps; the black swans on the river.

'You made a garden at Laudi didn't you?' asked Rolls.

'I found a garden there,' the Marchesa answered. 'I kept it.'

'You loved it didn't you?'

'It was a little green jewel,' said the Marchesa. 'It sufficed.'

Now Lark, Rollo supposes, is asleep. How can she sleep? I have avoided her of course, but then she also has avoided me. We have avoided one another, but how can she sleep? Surely she doesn't mean to end it there? Surely, we must at least be going to say 'Good-bye.' We haven't *arranged* anything, cries Rollo. There is so much to arrange. But she appears to be asleep in that room that is the nursery. Behind the curtains with the fiddling mice, level with the top branches of the plane-tree. How can she sleep?

Lark only sees those branches change eleven times – bud; the leaves turn green; turn dry; fall and drift away leaving the branches bare to bud again – eleven times against Selina's seventy, Griselda's twenty-three, and the fifty-nine that are to be given to Grizel. Eleven in comparison is a slight number but Lark does not claim a presence as the others do; only a presence through Rollo, through Roly and Rollo and Rolls, whom she loves. In the vision, if Rollo had followed it, she belongs to him and the garden that presages her need not be foreign and unseen; it is his; his are the groves and the river and the bounding dog; even the hat is not like a hat in a vision, it is chosen and bought and paid for by him; she is his; and now, walking in the Place with his shadow, he sees that again and as he sees it, he is filled with such consummate bliss that his guard falls down and with it his prudence and his fears. 'Good God my God!' says Rollo. 'What a fool I have been!' He comes bounding up the steps just in time to prevent Proutie from bolting the door.

Young Proutie is in a brown dressing-gown. 'Proutie! Not in bed?'

'I had a feeling about the door,' says Proutie. 'I thought maybe I hadn't put the chain up, so I came down and found the door wide open.'

'I did that, not you,' says Rollo.

'You haven't been to bed.' Proutie's eyes, blue tell-tale eyes, are wide and sympathetic. 'You wouldn't get *me* into the Army, Mr Rollo, not with all this serving overseas and wars.'

'When I let them put me into the Army, Proutie, I thought all wars were over,' says Rollo. He does not sound depressed now, he sounds hilarious and Proutie peers at him in the dimness of the hall. 'Proutie, you are going to do something for me.'

'Of course Mr Rollo. Anything.'

'Go up to the nursery and wake Miss Lark. Go very quietly and wake her and ask her to come down. Make her come down. Tell her it is important and urgent. And Proutie . . .'

'Yes sir?'

'It *is* important and urgent.'

Proutie goes and Rollo waits in the hall. The candles have burned down. There is only one left on the stairs and it burns low, shedding light only around itself; but it shows a glimpse, circled, of blue walls, cream banisters, serpentine rail. The house is filled with tickings, especially from the big clock near at hand, the grandfather. There is a scurry and rustle in the basement; a stair creaks but it is not Proutie coming down. What an age, an age is Proutie. Rollo strains and cannot hear a sound.

He walks to the drawing-room door; back again; close to the clock; he looks down into the blackness of the basement; up the stairs; there is not a sound.

The street door is still open and the Place, as it shows beyond its arch, pale, lighted by the lamps, is imprinted on Rollo's mind forever. Proutie comes running down the stairs ...

'Where is she? Proutie, won't she come?'

'Miss Lark is not in her room,' says Proutie, his tell-tale eyes astonished. 'Her bed hasn't been slep' in. There is a note for Mr Pelham, Mr Rollo. She is gone!'

'It is so peaceful to talk to you now,' said the Marchesa. 'Those questions, and actions, were like thorns and wounds in our minds. You hurt me so I hurt you. But that is all over. It is so peaceful to talk to you now.'

'I love you Lark. I love you. How much I love you, Lark.'

The candles are burning quietly along the walls; they shine on the gold in the barley-sheaves and poppies in the paper, on the picture frames, on the gilding of the chairs exactly as they did before; they are reflected quietly in the polished piano lid, in the tables, in the mirror; none of them have burst into torches; the shepherdess on the clock is still dreaming and the hands of the clock have only imperceptibly moved; the bronze chrysanthemums in the Chinese bowls are as they were: they have not hung themselves in garlands nor in wreaths. 'Then?' says Lark wonderingly. 'Then? And now?'

'*What are you thinking of?*'

'*Of us of course.*'

'*How we shall always be in love?*'

'*How we shall always be in love.*'

'*Even when we are old?*'

'*Even when we are old.*'

There was a shock of impact and noise and the glass of the window was blown in, straight in Rollo's face. The drawing-room wall sagged inwards, covering him as he fell. The balcony and steps rose up and tore away into the garden in an uprising of bricks and earth. The house shuddered to its foundations. The bomb had fallen on the garden wall between the lines of houses. The house on either side of it seemed to sway apart, but it was the house in Wiltshire Crescent that fell, hidden in a cloud of dust. Number 99 still stood.

Presently the All Clear sounded.

In this hour the outside sounds had lessened and the din of the guns died down. The searchlight had ceased to play over the sky, and behind the branches of the plane-tree the stars showed.

The garden was full of rubble and broken glass and dirt. The steps lay at an angle. The creepers, torn loose, swayed and stirred. There was a dead silence.

But the house was not silent; nor dead.

'*We thought it was going to end to-night, but it isn't. It is going to live.*'

'*I am the house dog.*'

'*I am the house cat.*'

'*They eat Larks in Italy.*'

'*I should like never to see our own dining-room again.*'

Chick chick chick chick chick chick
Lay a little egg for me.

'*Ultimately just.*'
'*Is it so important to be loved?*'
'*I should prefer it to be my own thigh.*'
'*We are having a lovely party.*'
'*You understand about the soubise?*'
No. 6. Valse. See-Saw. (Brown eyes?)
'* . . . at Char-asiab and Kabul and Kandahar.*'
'*A lease of occupation.*'
'*When did you grow up like this?*'
'*Why not be truthful, Grizel?*'
'*You must learn to read, you little dunce.*'

Ah – ahahahahahah – ah
Ah – ahahahahahah – ah . . .

'*Do not disturb me. I don't want to be disturbed.*'
'* . . . as your sister. Do you understand?*'
'*Come back. Come back. Elizabeth!*'
'*Real snow, Grizel.*'
'*Come Juno. We must go to bed.*'
'*How do you pronounce Popocatepetl?*'
'*Heliotrope, and they call it cherry-pie.*'

And the house continues in its tickings, its rustlings, its creakings; the ashes will fall in its grates, its doorbells ring; trains will pass under it and their sounds vibrate; footsteps will run up the stairs, along passages; dusters will be shaken, carpets beaten, beds turned down and dishes washed; windows will be opened and shut; blinds pulled up, pulled down; the tap will run and be silent; the lavatory will be flushed; the piano will be played and books taken down from the shelf; brushes will be lifted up and laid down again on the dressing-table: the medicine bottle will be shaken and flowers arranged in a vase; children will perhaps play spillikins and perhaps they will not; but mice, for mice will be mice and their fashions do not change, mice will run in the wainscot and the family will set traps for them. 'In me you exist,' says the house.

VIRAGO MODERN CLASSICS

The first Virago Modern Classic, *Frost in May* by Antonia White, was published in 1978. It launched a list dedicated to the celebration of women writers and to the rediscovery and reprinting of their works. Its aim was, and is, to demonstrate the existence of a female tradition in literature, and to broaden the sometimes narrow definition of a 'classic'. Published with new introductions by some of today's best writers, the books are chosen for many reasons: they may be great works of literature; they may be wonderful period pieces; they may reveal particular aspects of women's lives; they may be classics of comedy, storytelling, letter-writing or autobiography.

'The Virago Modern Classics list contains some of the greatest fiction and non-fiction of the modern age, by authors whose lives were frequently as significant as their writing. Still captivating, still memorable, still utterly essential reading' **SARAH WATERS**

'The Virago Modern Classics list is wonderful. It's quite simply one of the best and most essential things that has happened in publishing in our time. I hate to think where we'd be without it' **ALI SMITH**

'The Virago Modern Classics have reshaped literary history and enriched the reading of us all. No library is complete without them' **MARGARET DRABBLE**

'The writers are formidable, the production handsome. The whole enterprise is thoroughly grand' **LOUISE ERDRICH**

'Good news for everyone writing and reading today'
HILARY MANTEL